The Raja of Bourbon

Michel de Gréce

Translated from French
by
Sadaf Raza

LOTUS COLLECTION
ROLI BOOKS

Lotus Collection 2011

This translation first published in 2011
The Lotus Collection
An imprint of Roli Books Pvt. Ltd.
M-75, Greater Kailash II Market, New Delhi 110 048
Phone: ++91 (011) 4068 2000. Fax: ++91 (011) 2921 7185
E-mail: info@rolibooks.com; Website: www.rolibooks.com
Also at Bangalore, Chennai, Jaipur, Mumbai and Varanasi

Le Rajah Bourbon was first published by JC Lattés, Paris, © 2007 by Editions JC Lattés

Published in association with the French Embassy in India.

Cover Design: Divya Bhardwaj
Layout: Sanjeev Mathpal
Production: Shaji Sahadevan

ISBN: 978-81-7436-806-5

Typeset in Centaur MT by Roli Books Pvt Ltd
and printed at Anubha Printers, Noida, UP

Contents

Preface

Bhopal, November 2005

I had dreamed of going to Sanchi, the jewel in the crown of Buddhist art, for a long time. Photographs showed enormous stupas with gates adorned with the most delicate sculpture in the middle of the countryside. This art combined the abstraction of spirituality with the refinements of a poetic mythology. Sanchi is situated in central India, approximately mid-way between Delhi and Bombay, a region still not developed for tourists.

Friends advised me against spending the night there, the hotel industry being more or less primitive. However, Bhopal, a large city only fifty kilometres away, catered to my standard of comfort. The old capital of an independent principality ruled by rich Muslim nawabs, Bhopal is today the capital of the vast state of Madhya Pradesh, and has excellent hotels. Bhopal, for me, like for most of the world, remains darkly associated with the horrifying accident at Union Carbide, and the fatal gas leak which took thousands of lives in 1980. Despite this discouraging reference, the city won me over at first sight. A number of lakes marked its irregular design; colossal decrepit palaces stood on lush green hills. Tall, slender minarets in pink stone accentuated the old city. In the residential quarter, a street lined with palm trees leads to the Jahan Numah Palace hotel, one of the older residences of the nawabs, built in the beginning of the twentieth century. I was struck by its lush gardens, the grass impeccably mown, the long white galleries open to the skies and old photographs of exotic sovereigns.

A smiling employee escorted me upstairs to a mahogany door. As he was opening the door, my eyes glanced upon a sleek bronze plate that had engraved upon it: 'The Bourbon Suite'. I had already noticed in passing a 'Godard Suite', a 'Senator Jeffrey Suite', and other names of Western origin. But why the name 'Bourbon' in the middle of central India? When I asked the employee about it, he advised me to ask the concierge.

'Why Bourbon? Very simple,' the concierge replied, 'because it is the name of one of the most prestigious families of Bhopal, a very old family which has played a prominent role in the history of this region and is the subject of a number of legends.'

I rephrased my question, 'So how does this family happen to bear the name Bourbon?' Typically Indian, the concierge refused to admit that he didn't know anything and proposed to arrange a meeting with the head of the family, whom I could question at leisure. He glanced through the telephone directory and read to me, 'Bourbon Balthazar, 8 Church Road, Jahangirabad'. He added, 'It is the address of the school which is run by the family, the Bourbon School.' He dialed the number. I heard him say, 'Mr Bourbon, I have here a French tourist (I don't know him) who would like to meet you.' A murmur followed. The director hung and turned to me, 'He will see you in one hour.'

We left the hotel at dusk. The Indian road, ruled by intense chaos by day, now turns to outright pandemonium. In the semi-darkness, entire walls of bicycles, mopeds, vespas speed towards us, goats, buffaloes, camels walk freely, families chat on the asphalt, children cross the road without any regard to safety, and sadhus, the skeletal holy men wrapped in saffron, move between cars as if they didn't exist.

The driver was not from Bhopal, yet we reached the popular quarter of Jahangirabad without much difficulty. We asked for directions many times; everyone knew The Bourbon School, but some explanations are such that several times they sent us on the wrong route. Finally, we were set on the right road that wound between violently lit shops. On my right, I saw a large building left in darkness with an enormous board, The Bourbon School.

As the gates opened we entered a huge dark, shadowy courtyard. A rather small, portly man with a moustache and a smile appeared and announced, 'I am Balthazar de Bourbon.' He took me to another courtyard in the middle of which stood a modern villa, enclosed by a small garden. Next to the door, underneath an enormous metal fleur de lys was engraved in tall letters in golden bronze, 'House of Bourbon'. Balthazar's family was waiting for me: his wife Elisha and their three children, Frédéric, aged twenty, Michele, aged seventeen, and the youngest, Adrien.

We entered a living room with high ceilings. In typically Indian fashion, the temperature inside was freezing. Everyone took a seat on huge armchairs. They observe me with curiosity, with warmth, but also perhaps a dash of suspicion. Acutely embarrassed, I began to explain myself. 'I have just discovered that a family in Bhopal bore the name Bourbon, which happens to be the name of my mother as well (Bourbon Orleans maybe, but Bourbon all the same). I don't mean to be indiscreet, but I simply wanted to find out by what coincidence you bear this family name.' In response, Balthazar left the room and soon returned with an old, visibly worn-out volume, held together by strips of scotch tape. I glanced at the back of the book: Louis Rousselet, *L'Inde et ses rajahs,* 1875. The book opened almost of its own accord to a particular page that Balthazar made me read:

> Bhopal 1865. One day while smoking hukkas and savouring sorbets at a gathering that I was invited to, a powerful voice surprised me by announcing: "Padri Sahib, the head priest." A minute later I saw enter into the room a young man dressed in a catholic priest's clothes. The entire gathering stood up, for the Muslims always show the greatest respect for our ecclesiastical costume. I went forward to the priest who to my great surprise addressed me in French ... What luck! A Frenchman in Bhopal! When everyone sat down, the missionary spoke to me: "On hearing about your arrival, I was eager to come see you as it has been a long time since I had the pleasure of meeting a fellow countryman, but I had to delay my visit for a reason that you will easily understand. I reside here in my capacity as the chaplain of Madam Elisabeth de Bourbon, a Christian princess who is in the first position in the kingdom after the Begum. The princess really hoped that you would come see her as soon as you arrived; she

has been awaiting you impatiently. Being but a servant, I had to postpone my visit till the day she authorized me to come find you. I have come today, sent by her, to convey that she will wait for you in her palace, tomorrow, at a time that is convenient to you." I was listening to the priest talk to me but I could not believe my ears. My journey had already offered me unexpected surprises, but coming to Bhopal to find a French chaplain to a Christian princess, to learn that this princess is one of the most important figures in the country, and that she bears the name Bourbon, all this seemed to be touch by the surreal to me, and I looked at the nice priest, wondering if underneath all this there wasn't a mystery. Finally, I accepted the invitation of the mysterious princess, and he left us to deliver the news to her.

When he left, I questioned the noble Bhopalis present there, and they confirmed what the priest had said. The princess was commonly known la Doulan Sircar, which means the Queen of the betrotheds, a nickname that she came to merit some fifty years ago, for she now counted some seventy summers; but her real name was Bourbon Sircar, meaning the princess of Bourbon. It is also true that she used to be very rich, possessing important territories and occupying the first rank amongst the great nobles of the crown.

My curiosity was strongly awakened. So the next morning I mounted an elephant and was led towards the palace of the princess. We stopped in front of a palace of modest appearance but enormous dimensions, and were received by a large number of armed servants who, after having helped us descend our elephant, led us to a big room situated on the first floor, where the Doulan Sircar was waiting for us. The princess shook our hands warmly. Her face struck me, the European character of which was even more enhanced by the fairness of her skin. Did I really have in front of me a compatriot, and by what bizarre string of circumstances did she find herself here, in Bhopal, in a position so high? After having undergone the customary interrogation, which the princess did not spare me from, I questioned her in my own turn and received from her the most curious information about the origin of her family....

> In the seventeenth century, a European arrived in India by the name of Jean de Bourbon….

We were interrupted by Elisha de Bourbon and her children who announced that snacks were being served. We moved on to a vast dining room decorated by an enormous aquarium and an even bigger refrigerator. The snack – in fact a huge meal – looked delicious, a succession of curries, each more delightful than the other followed by irresistible pastries. On the other hand, there was not a drop of wine, only fruit juice. I could not help but remark, 'Dear Balthazar, it is not really in the traditions of the Bourbons to not like wine.' He burst into a frank and infectious laugh and said, 'To tell you the truth, my ancestors were quite the drunkards, and so my grandfather made us vow never to touch alcohol.' I asked about him and his family: he was a lawyer in the court; his wife Elisha looked after the Bourbon school founded by his family. His elder son, pleasant and open, was a documentary filmmaker. While the other two children were still in school. I looked with interest at the five members of this hospitable and smiling family. They were typically, profoundly and exclusively Indian, and yet they bore the prestigious and very French name Bourbon.

I asked Balthazar if he possessed any family archives and above all if they led to the legendary Jean de Bourbon. His descendant shook his head sadly. 'I couldn't find anything, I have not a single original paper. All that could have existed has disappeared.' Over the course of our conversation, I discovered that his knowledge of the French monarchy, the House of France, of the family branch of the Bourbons was more than limited. I was surprised that he himself, his parents or his grandparents never researched this side of things. 'My parents never had the time. And I inherited heavy responsibilities very early in life. My father died when I was eighteen years old, leaving me to take care of my mother and four sisters to marry, as well as his law firm. During these years I had to shoulder my responsibilities amongst the worst difficulties. I never had the leisure to do any research.'

'How come you never went to France, even as a tourist?' I asked.

'Precisely because with a name like this, I can never go simply as a tourist. One of my sisters went to France a few years ago, she wanted to visit a castle that belonged to the Bourbons but was closed to the public. She took out her Indian passport with the name Bourbon in it and the guards let her in.'

The prestigious name is inscribed on all their identity papers, as it is inscribed on their visiting cards, their schools, their houses, their birthday, wedding and funeral invitations, everywhere Bourbon, everywhere the fleurs de lys on their buildings, on their letter heads. I understood that they were obsessed with this past that they had no way of accessing and yet from which they could not escape.

I asked Balthazar if Jean, the legendary ancestor, has many descendants: 'In the past, we were a clan of around four hundred families, of which three hundred were settled in Bhopal. But now everyone has migrated to Europe, to Australia, to New Zealand. I am now the only Bourbon still living in India, in fact in all Asia.'

I couldn't help but ask, 'Why did your cousins leave Bhopal?'

'We had problems, big problems,' he replied.

I didn't dare insist, for I realized that Balthazar was not going to say anything more. Yet, I was intrigued to find out why all the Bourbons of Bhopal, excepting him, had suddenly migrated. Balthazar eluded the questions that I had prepared to ask him. 'My cousins have left behind them here the most precious thing: their deceased ones. Come and see.' He led me to the road. A few hundreds of metres from his compound stood in the darkness a massive church. 'It is my ancestor, Princess Isabelle, of whom Rousselet wrote, who constructed this in the middle of the nineteenth century.'

As we entered the church, it lit up. The sanctuary was very simple, very plain. Balthazar vigorously pushed aside the benches to clear the gravestones in marble inlaid on the floor. 'Isabelle de Bourbon', 'Bonaventure de Bourbon', 'Sebastien de Bourbon'. There were a dozen.

The moment of goodbyes had come. Whether because of discretion or decency, Balthazar did not ask me, but I could tell he'd like me to help him discover the truth. So who was this Jean de Bourbon who came to India in the sixteenth century? Himself, Balthazar, was he or was he not related to the dynasty of the Bourbons, and thus to the House of France? The mystery intrigued me enough; so much so that I promised him I would do all the necessary research and send him news, even if it turns out to be negative and therefore disappointing.

I returned to the hotel extremely baffled, but convinced that the answer, the key to the mystery was to be found not in India, but in France.

As soon as I was back, I began the promised research. It let me discover that I was not the first one to be interested in the Bourbons of India. Ever since the exposure by Rousselet in his *Inde des Rajahs,* scattered researchers have been inclined towards this case. Many hypotheses have been developed on the identity of this Jean de Bourbon, each one more implausible than the other.

I went back to Louis Rousselet, the French traveller who had named himself the 'discoverer' of the Bourbons of Bhopal.

After the wonderful success of his *Inde des Rajahs,* first published in 1875, he published a second edition in 1879, but oddly enough there he added, in relation to his meeting with Princess Isabelle de Bourbon, an important and unedited paragraph, and I wondered what could have inspired him to do so.

From this detail onwards, I was involved on a winding, often tricky trail, which, whether marked by clues or deductions, was imbedded in the shadows of history.

1516

'MY cousin, my true friend, it is to you that I owe this victory and I want all present here to know that.' King François I expressed in a strong and manly voice. It was in a hesitant tone that the Commander replied, 'Sire, you honour me far too much, it was you and you alone, who led your army to victory. You fought, Sire, not just like a king, but like a heroic warrior. Your horse was injured twice but even that failed to budge you.'

'And you, cousin, weren't you at times, during the battle, surrounded by enemies, as I have noted in the report? You fought like a charging wild boar, without a thought for your skin. And it is to your qualities as Chief of the Army, above all, that I pay homage this evening. You organized an espionage service that informed us of the movements of the enemy. You succeeded in pushing back the Swiss who wanted to seize our artillery. You led a furious attack against them, which forced them to recede. If ever the name Marignan should ring in the history of France, it will be associated with you, Commander of Bourbon.'

The King's speech echoed under the gothic vaulting of the grand hall of the Chateau de Moulins. On his return from Italy where he had been victorious, François I decided to honour his cousin by stopping at his home. The general staff, the French Court and the barely-less numerous dukes of Bourbon reunited for the festivities. The campaign was over for the year, and austerity no longer in fashion. Men competed with the women in their multi-hued velvets and silks. The feathers that adorned their brocade berets were their decorations whereas heavy jewels covered the necks and hair of the women of the court.

The guests had their eyes turned towards the two men, the King François I, and his cousin, the Commander of Bourbon. Both were young: while the King was twenty-five years old, the Commander was twenty-seven. Both of them were exceptionally tall for the time: the King was almost two metres tall, and Bourbon more than 1.85 metres. Both were handsome and immensely popular with the ladies. The King with his almond eyes, soft expression, and voluptuous smile, was a charmer. The non-existent chin hidden by the beard betrayed any weakness of character. The Commander, with a Herculean build, maintained a more grave expression. He had inherited dark eyes from his Italian mother. His attitude betrayed an indomitable personality. His physique was in striking contrast to that of his wife, Suzanne, the Duchess of Bourbon. She was small, petite and slightly distorted, with one shoulder higher than the other, which led one to guess at a weak constitution. And yet, her expression radiated goodness, generosity and love. She listened, with her luminous and frank smile, to the compliments showered on her by her neighbour on the table, Louise de Savoie, Countess of Angouleme, mother of the King François I.

The two women were first cousins. Louise's mother was a Bourbon – but fifteen years separated them. Suzanne was twenty-five years old, Louise about forty. She had almond eyes like her son the King, but a hooked nose, an indecipherable expression, and her incessantly staring look gave her the appearance of a shrew. She congratulated her cousin Suzanne over the Commander's success, and Suzanne was full of praise for the valiance of the young King. The two women also talked about the fears they had felt, the one for her son, the other for her husband, during the bloody war. It was what they had suffered during the absence of their beloveds that drew them together. Just like their beloved, currently praising each other's exploits during the campaign, they too were linked by an unbreakable friendship.

After the death, two years earlier, of the old fogy Louis XII, an old, sickly and lewd man, King François I began a reign of youth, adventure, action, and pleasure. A young and dynamic generation had come to power with him who dreamt of heroic battles and passionate love. He was eager to grant his favourite cousin, Charles de Bourbon the Commander's sword, the highest military distinction in the kingdom, and sure enough took him to the Italian wars where his youthful ardour made him a conqueror. Meanwhile, the gilded youth loved to entertain himself, and found the most refined recreation worthy of his expectations in the Chateau de Moulins. The residence of the dukes of Bourbon was by far the most beautiful in France, far more luxurious than the palace of the King in Paris, the old-fashioned Louvre. The Commander's invitees to the Marignan fete were impressed by the formidable ramparts, the imposing towers, and seduced by the massive black lava-stone fountain that stood in the middle of the vast courtyard. While visiting the apartments, they admired the tapestry from Flanders that formed the most exquisite collection in Europe, the carpets from the Orient, other impressive examples of the goldsmith's art, and the elaborate furniture. They lingered in the dungeon called Le Mal Coiffé, which also sheltered the ducal library, one of the richest in the world. In the gardens that descended to the Allier, they walked between the pine trees, the laurels, orange trees, lemon trees, hazel trees, and breathed in the perfume of flowers of the most diverse type and the most perfumed. They were enraptured by the marvel that was the enormous fountain in gleaming bronze that represented a giant artichoke. They were lost in the green labyrinth where they discovered rare birds enclosed in large decorated cages and animals brought from far away lands that inhabited the menagerie. They had, to fulfil their slightest wish, hundreds of servants wearing the ducal uniform, distinguished gentlemen, squires, chamberlains, cupbearers, ushers, and the harbinger of arms, doctors. Chaplains were at the ready, watching out for their souls.

Before supper, the invitees had the time to admire in this architectural jewel that was the Saint-Louis chapel, the huge alter piece made by an anonymous genius who would pass through history under the name Maitre de Moulin. It represented the Virgin and child surrounded by its donators on their knees, the parents of Suzanne de Bourbon, the parents-in-law of the Commander, the sire of Beaujeu, dead for the past ten years, and his wife, the formidable Anne de

Beaujeu. The latter was the favourite daughter of Louis XI, King of France and a great genius, who saw him in herself.

She presided over the table of the king this evening. She excluded herself from the general good cheer. Laughter, joie de vivre was not natural to this matchless politician of a very profound spirit. A large and domed forehead revealed a brain of exceptional capacity. A very small nose and heavy eyelids didn't make for beauty in this rich fifty-year-old woman. Her eyes were creased to the point where one would think them closed. And yet, the sharp dagger-like look of Anne de Beaujeu did not miss a moment or a detail. And what she saw gave her even less reason to smile. Without being obvious, she observed Louise de Savoie, the King's mother, who was affectionately chatting with her daughter Suzanne. She knew that Louise, her niece, had hated her since adolescence. It was, in fact Anne de Beaujeu who took her in when she lost her parents at a very young age. Louise was brought up in the very austere court of the Bourbons. She believed herself to have been treated like a poor cousin and she held it against her aunt. She never forgave her for being married off, no sooner had she been of age, to an old debauched man thirty years her elder, the Count of Angouleme, who had openly cheated on her with his mistress, and left her a widow at the age of eighteen. That Louise hated her did not perturb Anne the dowager, a woman of power, the longtime regent of France for her brother Charles VIII when he was still a minor. She was well accustomed to provoking hatred due to her energy and natural authority. What did worry her was the nature of this Louise that she was beginning to discover. The King's mother, however, was a past master in the art of secrecy, and hypocrisy was her favourite weapon. But Anne, who saw through souls, knew her to be cruel, rapacious, devious, greedy, jealous, and ready to do anything to get what she wanted. Now, Anne knew that Louise ferociously desired the enormous fortune of the Bourbons, an impressive addition of counts, dukes, principalities and rulers.

To crown it all, the greedy Louise had solid arguments to permit herself this dream, being the only first cousin of Suzanne and her closest relative. If Suzanne died without a child, Louise would inherit. Of course, there was Suzanne's husband, the Commander.

But Louise, at the bottom of her heart, felt she had more right to inheritance than him.

Of course, everything would have changed if Suzanne and the Commander have had children. Anne de Beaujeu looked at her only child with affection and sadness, this Suzanne, so nice, her soul so radiant, but the body so fragile, so frail, so unsuitable for conception and childbirth. For ten years now, she had been married to the magnificent Commander. What was more, they loved each other deeply. The Commander, contrary to an enormous majority of princes and gentlemen, had never had a mistress. Keeping himself away from women, he stayed completely devoted to his fairly unattractive wife. He respected her and he loved her. And yet, in ten years of marriage, the couple had never succeeded in having a child. They probably never would, and hence the path was open for the cruel intrigues and greed of Louise. She had already begun to distil poison into the relationship between the Commander and her son, the King. The two cousins embraced one another and swore eternal friendship, but this war had already provoked some serious friction. For this conquest of Italy crowned by the victory at Marignan, the Bourbons had spent hundreds of thousands of pounds to arm and maintain the King's troops. The government, however, was in no hurry to reimburse them. It was Anne de Beaujeu herself who sent a reminder to the government. The chancellor of France, a creation of Louise's, sent a message that he did not have the means, and suggested that the wealth displayed by the Bourbons on this precise evening of victory, allowed them to survive easily without the reimbursement of the debt.

The dowager Anne seethed with rage, much like her son-in-law, the Commander, to see lords who fought far less than him, who served their King far less, receive pensions and benefits, while he himself got nothing more than verbal compliments. King François I was at heart a good man, but everyone knew that he was completely dominated by his mother. And Louise was decided on creating animosity between her son and the Bourbons, and she had already started to act secretly towards this goal.

Under her heavy eyelids, the eyes of the dowager Anne searched out Louise. She was no more in her place. Next to her daughter

Suzanne was now seated the lovely queen Claude, wife of King François. She had a wonderful nature, a generous heart, but was incapable of keeping an adulated and fickle husband. Aptly, he was flirting with his latest official mistress, the very beautiful Madame de Chateaubriant as they danced, which allowed them to come closer, for the ball had begun. In the gallery, the viola and tambourine players of the private orchestra of the dukes of Bourbon played dance after dance. So where had Louise gone? She spotted her twirling around with the Commander. She was always well dressed in the black of a widow, and Anne knew her to be coquettish. The dowager's eyes screwed up even more as she watched her dreadful niece as though she would like to pierce her with her eyes. And suddenly Anne was shocked for she could not believe what she was seeing. Louise, the King's mother, was looking with adoration at the Commander, with whom she was dancing. There was no mistake. The eyes of her niece betrayed her passion almost absolutely. It could not be but a demonic manoeuver or perhaps a passing infatuation. Perhaps this evening, the King's mother was drunk. However, that too was impossible, concluded the dowager Anne, Louise was well in complete control of herself. Widowed for more than twenty years, she had never been known for any adventure, for giving in to any temptation. She had always taken care of this appearance of austerity. So what was this demon that had taken over her?

1517

No one could believe it: Suzanne, the duchess of Bourbon, the wife of the Commander, was finally pregnant. Her delicate body, her frail constitution and ten years of infertility had indicated that she was incapable of giving birth, though it was critical that she give birth to an inheritor. In the middle of summer, the duchess delivered. To everyone's surprise, she did not die of puerperal fever, and the child too survived. To top it all, she gave birth to a son. Henceforth it was this child who was to be the inheritor of this shower of dukedoms, principalities, lordships, and the baronies of his parents. The subjects of the duchy were overcome with joy, chanting the Te Deum of thanksgiving with banquets and improvised balls.

The baptism of the inheritor was to take place with pomp and ceremony. The baby was already titled the Count of Clermont and an armed knight. He was to be baptized by the bishop of Lisieux. The King of France, François I accepted the role of godfather. He visited Moulins again for the event. In order to receive him with dignity the Commander organized numerous wonderful shows. Simulacrum of battles, tournaments, confrontations with monsters, all these warlike shows were produced on a grand scale. The baptism of the baby took place in the marvelous Saint-Louis chapel of the Moulins castle. The King, dressed in black and white – his favourite colours – was standing on one side of the baptismal font. On the other, holding the baby and facing him was the godmother, the duchess dowager, Anne, Suzanne's mother. She went grandiosely through the long ceremonial rites and perfectly played the role of godmother. This, however, did not stop her from constantly thinking: in front of her, the King seemed perfectly happy and yet the birth of this child, of whom he was the godfather, was a catastrophe, for it took away from him and his mother the possibilities of getting their hands on the enormous inheritance of the Bourbons. The dowager could not help but let slip a smile across her thin lips, thinking of the disappointment and the anger of the King's mother at the idea of seeing such a gigantic fortune escape her. She would have loved to know what was going on in the mind of this detestable and appalling niece of hers. Under her lowered eyelids, she looked for Louise. There she was, very close. She did not at all have a sullen air about her, and was displaying, on the contrary an ecstatic expression, and despite all the hypocrisy that she was capable of, the dowager could sense that Louise was not putting it on. She was visibly full of joy and her eyes did not leave the Commander. The baby nearly slipped out of the duchess's hands into the baptismal font. But how could this be! Louise was still in love with Anne's son-in-law! Not only was she still in love, she was even more in love than before. During the banquet that followed, she pursued him almost openly, not leaving him even for a second in peace, placing herself always by his side, trying to engage him in conversation, throwing him the blazing glances of an adorer swooning with happiness. The forty year old dressed in black risked herself for her beloved with simpers and coyness that the dowager never believed her to be capable of. The Commander pretended not to be aware of any of it. He was too courteous to put the King's mother in her place. But his dark eyes flashed in anger: he was not going to yield to the absurd passion of Louise. Anne also knew that her son-in-law never believed in compromises and half-measures. She wondered how he was going to handle this impossible situation. She also worried about Louise's reaction, for she was not one to abandon her crush. Louise, who was the opposite of spontaneity, romanticism, of voluptuousness was so madly and irreparably in love with the Commander: the 'She-Monkey', as Duchess Anne called her niece Louise had become crazy about the young sapling. The Commander was twenty-eight years old, but for

Anne, he would always be a sapling. The she-monkey mad about the sapling, what an embarrassment! For Louise would crush ferociously and without pity all who dared oppose her will and her desires.

The dowager pulled herself together to reply to the strident voice of the bishop who asked her what name the baby would bear. 'He shall be named François,' like the King, his godfather, and thus his protector.

1519

Little François, Count of Clermont, son of Suzanne and the Commander, died after a brief illness at the age of one. His parents and his grandmother were in despair. Once again, the future of the inheritance of the dukes of Bourbon was in suspense.

The Commander and Suzanne tried again. Suzanne was pregnant once again. She delivered twins, boys ... stillborn.

1521

Suzanne was pregnant for the third time ... and the last. Her constitution, further weakened by the previous pregnancies could not take another. However, she wanted to leave him an inheritor at any cost, even if that cost were to be her life. Slowly and progressively as the delivery came closer, the anxiety built up in the family and in the entourage of the lovely Duchess Suzanne. Everyone was gathered at the Moulins castle when, one autumn evening, the labour began. Hours passed and the delivery turned out to be difficult. The Commander at this point was so nervous that his mother-in-law, the Duchess Anne, sent him to the castle's chapel. He knelt on the hard, cold stone floor, and looking at the statue of the gently smiling Virgin, prayed with all his heart. He prayed more for his wife than for the child to be born. He wanted her to live, and too bad if he weren't to have an heir. His fevered pleas were mixed with bitter thoughts in which the King François and his mother appeared. The King took pleasure in humiliating his cousin who had shown him nothing but loyalty and devotion. It was to others that he gave important posts; it was others whom he allows his confidences. As for his mother, Louise, the very idea of the woman who very indiscreetly displayed her passion for him was repulsive and disgusting. He never wanted to see her again. Lost in his thoughts at the moment, even though he should have been on guard, he did not hear the door of the chapel open ....

'... A stillborn son.' The news spread in the castle and messengers left to carry it to the court, to the King and his mother. 'A dead son is born... the last of his race ...'.

❧

Two weeks,... three weeks passed. Suzanne had not recovered from childbirth. She was suffering from a weakened and atrophied body. Her husband did not leave her bedside. With inexpressible sadness, he watched the life that he loved so much, slowly fade away like a candle. Suzanne still found the energy to turn towards him and look at him with all her affection, to smile at him and say a few words of comfort. Neither of them pretended anymore, they both knew that the end was close. 'My friend, she murmured, you must not remain alone in life. Too much menace surrounds you, too many worries burden you. I beg you, for the sake of my love, to remarry and have children.' In a fierce tone the Commander replied: 'My sweetheart, there was never anyone but you, and there will never ever be anyone but you.' He lay himself down on the quilt next to her, he took her hand into his and looked at her for a long time. He then leant and looked straight into her eyes. She smiled to which he responded with a similar smile. Despite the sadness of the moment, there was in their eyes, on their lips, a profound satisfaction, a complete bond, a sort of relief bathed in infinite love. She then closed her eyes and was asleep soon after. The Commander leant towards her and lightly touched her lips. God granted his servant Suzanne the grace to escape painful agony and to die in her sleep.

Her funeral took place with grand ceremony in the Pantheon of the dukes of Bourbon, in the abbey of Souvigny. Her mother, Anne de Beaujeu, with a waxen face and eyes almost entirely closed, remained impassive behind her black veil. Next to her, the Commander seemed, to the frivolous women of the Moulins court, even more handsome in his black velvet costume. And yet, the expression on his face at this point was so fierce and bitter that it frightened all those who looked at him. Suddenly, to everyone's surprise, the lines on his face seemed to soften into an incomprehensible grimace, and he collapsed in heavy sobs. Nobody could have ever imagined the Commander of Bourbon capable of an emotional explosion. The fit, instead of calming, increased into such a staggering and hiccupping fit that Charles withdraw to the sacristy. Anne de Beaujeu had not moved.

A month later, the widower was called to Paris, to the Louvre. The King received him in his most affectionate manner. He showed himself to be deeply saddened by the death of Suzanne and promised his cousin to do all he could to console him. He allotted to him one of the most beautiful apartments of the old palace. Every evening, he invited him to the parties he hosted. In spite of his mourning, the Commander felt obliged by courtesy to attend them. He felt miles away from the sumptuous and voluptuous spectacles that took place around him. François I protected him from too much attention. The mother of the King remained invisible. The Commander still did not know the reason behind this convocation.

Several days passed, and then, one spring morning, the Chancellor of France, Duprat, arrived at his apartment. This man, cunning, deceitful, devious, hungry with ambition, had no principles; no sense of modesty constrained him. He was the creation of Louise de Savoie who had herself placed him in such a key post. The chancellor began by expressing his condolences. Next, in a soft voice, he said: 'Would you, my lord, want to add to your already enormous possessions of Angoumois, Touraine, Anjou and Maine?'

The Commander was on his guard immediately. 'And by what miracle, Chancellor?'

'By simply accepting to marry Madam Louise de Savoie, widowed Countess of Angouleme, and the mother of our beloved King.'

In spite of all his self-control and his experience of things and people, the Commander was appalled. In a voice barely audible, he managed to murmur, head hanging low, eyes closed: 'You want me to marry a woman fifteen years older than me when my own wife is barely buried?'

'The mother of our King is definitely not at the peak of her youth. However, my lord, allow me to say that at forty-six years of age, she is more attractive than, despite her younger age, your late wife was,' the Chancellor replied.

'Mister Chancellor, if I were not staying at the King's palace, I would have thrown you out for this blasphemy. You should know that I have loved and I do love my wife, and that I feel nothing but repulsion for this person whom you want me to wed.'

The Chancellor pressed on, 'Think about it, my lord, reason imposes this marriage as the only solution to the problem of inheritance of your wife, the late Duchess.'

The Commander replied, 'My principles do not allow me to even consider what you are calling the only solution.'

The Chancellor then abandoned his polite tone for a threatening one: 'Madam Louise does not like resistance. Do not put yourself unnecessarily in danger, my lord.' The Commander had had enough, and decided to gain some time. 'In any case, the union that you propose to me remains unthinkable to the living mother of my wife, Anne the Duchess.' Without saying a word, the Chancellor bowed and left.

The very next day, lawyers of the Crown chosen and instructed by Chancellor Duprat asked the Commander Duke of Bourbon for the totality of the inheritance of his wife. At once, the Commander and his mother-in-law took the precautions that were called for. Duchess Anne wrote a will that left the entire inherited possessions of her daughter to her in-laws. As for the Commander, he made a will that left all his possessions to his mother-in-law, Duchess Anne.

The Parliament of Paris, the only court authorized to judge this affair, sent four investigating officers. The lawyers chosen by the Commander put themselves to the task. The Parliament, after several weeks of investigation, refused to grant satisfaction to the King's mother and adjourned the process. Chancellor Duprat, immediately arrested the four investigating officers nominated by the Parliament whose conclusions were in favour of the Duke of Bourbon.

1522

Anne de Beaujeu, dowager Duchess of Bourbon, mother of Suzanne and mother-in-law of the Commander, and by far the most powerful political face of France, was dead. She was soberly and simply buried in the abbey of Souvigny where her husband and daughter rested. As long as she had been alive, the formidable dowager, with her prestige, her personality, her power, had held back the sharks. Her death let them loose on the Commander, now without support. By a completely arbitrary act, François I seized the Commander's possessions. He gifted his mother the essentials, Bourbonnais and Auvergne. The Commander rightfully called this act a 'shameless theft' but was powerless to defend himself as no one dared support him. He remained alone in front of the unscrupulous and unrestrained.

1523

It was the height of summer and the Commander was sick, very sick. He was in his Moulins castle. By some unexpected sense of decency, he had not yet been evicted. He was incapable of leaving his bed; the fever had him confined to one place. He heard that François I was close to Moulins, en route to Lyon where he was returning to resume the war with Italy. The King stopped by the castle to greet his cousin. A curious visit, this one was quite different from the previous ones. Before arriving at the castle, François I besieged it and then seized the keys. He scanned the place where he had attended ceremonies that he would never forget and of which he was probably even jealous. What a change since then! The most beautiful pieces of the goldsmith's art had disappeared, probably stored away. The oriental carpets had been rolled up. Instead of a swarm of overzealous servants, he met only a few frightened menservants. The King felt the sadness that bathed this residence, which had until recently been devoted to pleasure. Going up the stairs, he entered the Commander's room, whom he found lying on his bed, pale and weak.

The two men remained alone face to face for this crucial meeting. They would have stayed allies if Louise de Savoie had not created animosity between them. They would have formed an invincible pair, capable of leading France to victory everywhere. They used to be friends, and neither of them wanted to accept the inevitable. They refused to accept that all in fact was lost between them. While the Commander was in a weak position; he was unwell, at the mercy of the ruler; Francois I was in a superior position but there were rules to be respected. It had been revealed by his mother, as well as by his own spies, that the Commander had come to an agreement with the worst enemy of France, the Emperor Charles Quint, that he was ready to change camp and enter the service of the latter. The disappointed would-be lover left nothing to chance, she had the Commander surrounded with spying eyes that reported to her all that was said and all that was happening there.

François did not know how to behave. He seemed embarrassed when he said, 'My cousin, you are well aware that I am ready to begin a war against the emperor. My army is better trained, and the artillery, thanks to you, is modern and equipped. I am sure to win. Your place remains next to me, come with me to fight in Italy.'

'Sire, you have only to look at me to realize that I am incapable of moving at the moment. If you do not believe me, ask my doctors.'

'I believe you, I believe you cousin,' the King hesitated to continue, 'however, certain people around me have conceived some suspicions about you. It even seemed that you were ready to abandon me by joining the enemy. Yet, my knight's honour didn't allow me to believe these accusations without proof. Moreover, my friendship with you has not changed. I still love you as I did ten years before, the day after Marignan. I cannot accuse you.' The Commander was pale, bloodless; he was beaded with fat drops of sweat because of the fever. His voice trembled as he responded to the King, 'You must know, Sire, that you do not have a more loyal servant than me. The rumours that you have heard are nothing more than inventions spread to alienate me from yourself.'

As a friendly gesture, François embraced the Commander, 'I never for one moment believed that a man as noble as you would conspire and have such disloyal plans.'

'The day you honoured me by appointing me the Commander of France, I had taken the oath, Sire, to obey you forever.'

The two men took each other's leave on these pleasant words, but François I left behind in Moulins a strong contingent of armed men. Just in case.

Two days later, while in convalescence the Commander wrote a moving letter to the King. He swore complete and absolute loyalty to him, on the condition that justice be granted to him, which meant the restoration of his inheritance. He sent his friend the bishop of Autun to carry the letter to François I who was in Lyon preparing for his campaign in Italy. In response, François I arrested the carrier of the missive, in spite of him being a bishop, and sent off his troops to bring the Commander to him, dead or alive.

The latter had also taken his precautions. He was informed, by his own spies in the court, of the orders given by the King. He decided not to be caught alive and fall into his hands, in other words, in the hands of Louise de Savoie. He knew what his arrest would signify. He would be dragged to court, and thanks to the high offices of the King's mother, condemned and executed. With hardly any time to gather gold and the jewels, he escaped one night in the beginning of September. The Duke of Bourbon, Commander of France and the King's cousin, was now clandestine. In order to lay a false trail, his horse and those of his following were shod back to front in order to make it seem as though they were entering the castle instead of leaving it. He learnt that a reward of ten thousand gold écus had been put on his head. The King's troops hunted them everywhere. He decided to reduce his following in order to make it more difficult to be traced. He and his men disguised themselves, one as a seigneur and the others as the servants and headed out towards the south in order to get to Spain. But arriving in Roussillon, they found that the frontier was very well guarded and they were obliged to change their destination. They went back up the Rhone, past Valence, missing being recognized several times. They escaped many ambushes, lived a thousand adventures, each more incredible than the other.

After a month of frantic wandering, they arrived near Besançon. Here on they were out of the reach of the King as they found themselves in the Empire's territory. Perhaps the secret treaty signed many months ago had been made public. Ever since the Commander had been on the receiving end of the attacks by François I and Louise de Savoie, Charles Quint, pleased with such a bargain, had not stopped singing siren's songs in order to try and convince him to abandon his ungrateful ruler and join him. It was his mother-in-law, Anne the Duchess, who gave him the ultimate advise before dying: Louise de Savoie never lets go of her prey, also he has no hope to expect from her son. The only solution was to abandon the latter and to ally himself with the emperor. He resolved to do so little after the death of his mother-in-law and offered his services to Charles Quint, who in exchange promised in writing, the hand of his sister Eleonore, the widow Queen of Portugal, a dowry of hundred thousand gold écus, and the restoration of all his property, which would be established as an independent kingdom. Effectively, the Commander accepted that France had to be torn apart for his profit. It was betrayal, pure and simple.

Abandoned, then attacked, looted by those to whom he had sworn his loyalty and whom he loved, instinctively, naturally, from the beginning: the King, the royal family, and his blood relation. Cornered, he allied himself to the enemy, without realizing that behind the man who was his cousin was a nation of people, and by changing camps, he was rebelling against these people. His indomitable and fierce character prevented him from making any compromise. His deep bitterness, as a result of the injustices of which he became a victim, pushed him into a fatal trap. In spite of all the reasons and the pressures that forced him to change camps, the Commander of Bourbon would remain in the eyes of posterity a traitor, probably the most magnificent traitor in history.

The Commander went across to the enemy; his accomplices were arrested and brought to court. One, however, was condemned to be beheaded: Saint-Vallier, who served him during the last dramatic months before the flight. Saint-Vallier's daughter went to demand mercy for her father from the King. He received her, and dazzled by her beauty, granted her her father's life, and she offered her body to him. Her name was Diane de Poitiers and she thus began a promising career.

1525

The war had begun. Led by François I, 30,000 French soldiers had entered Italy. Charles Quint had appointed the Commander as the Lieutenant General of the empire. He was ready to fight against his own compatriots. He changed his Bourbonnais motto 'Hope' that he bore until now on his arms for a motto that he created that represented for a long time his state of mind: 'Omnis spes in ferro': (All my hope lies in iron).

At the beginning of the year, the French besieged Pavie, the second most important city of the Milanese, with the key to Milan as the primary objective. The Commander, at the head of the imperial army, came to save the city. On a February night, the French succeeded in opening an important breech in the fortifications of Pavie with their artillery. The imperial army, which was defending the city walls, was massacred by the French artillery, and received the order to retreat. François I was led to believe that there was a stampede. He went in pursuit of the imperial army. This is what the Commander had wanted, hiding behind the folds in the ground. When the French were well inside the enemy lines, he launched his attack from behind. The French tried to resist but were soon overwhelmed. The Swiss, their allies, took flight instead of coming to the aid of François I, who fought like a hero from an earlier age. Attacked by the imperials, he struck with his sword, with a spear; he killed, was hit himself, thankfully superficially, and bled from minor injuries. He risked being killed by the enemy who now attacked in dozens. The two imperial generals, the Commander and the count of Lannoy, upon seeing the danger he was in came to his rescue. François I handed them his sword. For the French it was a complete disaster: they had lost ten thousand men, a number of their generals had been killed, and their king was imprisoned. Charles Quint turned twenty-five years of age on the day. The resounding victory that the Commander of Bourbon had achieved for him, the true craftsman of the French defeat, had made him the master of Europe.

François I was taken to the royal tent. Doctors treated and bandaged him. A sumptuous supper was served to him. The Commander gave him his serviette, as would have done the most respectful courtier. Ten years ago, in Marignan, the Commander had won a decisive victory for François I, who rewarded him with ingratitude of the blackest kind. In Pavie, he avenged that in the most brilliant and the most irreparable way.

1527

The Commander expected from Charles Quint gratitude in measure of the services given in Pavie, and above all, the guard of his prisoner, the King of France. But, perhaps justifiably, he was not given this responsibility. François I, on the orders of Charles Quint, was dispatched to Madrid, without the Commander being charged with the responsibility of his transfer. Charles Quint, while showering the Commander with compliments and favours, enticing him with fantastic promises, kept him confined in Italy, while in Spain, he engaged in negotiations with François I, leading to the Treaty of Madrid. François I ceded Bourgogne to the Emperor and other provinces which amputated France. The conqueror and the conquered vowed eternal friendship. In return, Charles Quint offered François I nothing less than his sister's hand in marriage, Eleonore, the widowed Queen of Portugal, the very same promised to the Commander in the secret treaty which had united them. The latter was also not forgotten in the new treaty. François I promised to return all the territories that were confiscated from him and to never again challenge his ownership. The King was freed from his prison, and as soon as he arrived in France, broke all the promises made in the Treaty of Madrid, starting with the ones concerning the Commander. 'I owe nothing to this traitor,' he argued. Charles Quint did not protest. Even though François I shamelessly refused to fulfil the commitments promised, he decided to maintain his relationship with him. Through treaties and their denunciations, through wars, victories and truces, Charles Quint had sealed a decisive dialogue with François I, and no one was going to affect that, least of all the Commander.

The latter finally understood that Charles Quint had used him from the beginning, that he was no longer required, and therefore had been dropped. To abandon the Emperor, to backtrack was too late; the Commander had come too far. He therefore remained officially in the service of the Emperor. On the other hand, he did not want to dismiss the army reunited with such great difficulty, which was loyal to him, and which he paid from now on with his own funds. To do that, it was necessary to find work for them, in other words a war. Knowing that the Commander was reduced to accepting any mission, the Emperor entrusted him with one that surely did require skill, but which at the end of the day was unworthy of the prime general of Europe. 'My dear Commander, I give you the responsibility of castigating the Pope Clement. It has been years since this damned Medici has been taking his pleasure by putting a spoke in my wheels. No matter what I do, he rebels against me. His intrigues have cost me considerable harm. This time, he has crossed his limits and I have decided to teach him a lesson, one that he and my other enemies will never forget. Go get Rome for me, and bring me the Pope Clement.'

To attack the holy city, to put a hand on Christianity's Pontiff, was something that in normal circumstances a French prince, a strategist of the Emperor, would have refused.

But Charles de Bourbon had become a condottiere, one of those knights of adventure who offer their military services to one or the other. They would be put at the head of troops by those who would assemble and pay them, to wage war wherever they were sent. No misgivings, neither pity nor piety contained them. These savages, crazy about lucre and debauchery, became the terror of Europe. The Commander was perfectly aware to what level he had stooped. He had believed that he was being called to play an important role in the European chessboard; he was forced to surrender to the evidence and accept the fact that he counted no more. He thus had nothing left to lose.

The Marquisat of Mantoue, 1527

Jean is six years old. With brown hair that is almost black, his almond shaped blue eyes, he looks a lot older than he actually is. Grown up fast, he is extremely thin in spite of a solid appetite. Like all children without parents, he matures faster. When dreams takes him to worlds only known to him, his expression is tinted with melancholy but also with depth, he seems to see things that others cannot see. But then, his eyes shine with excitement and joy as well, for he is passionately playing with the other boys of the village. What are they playing, apart from of course playing a war game, for isn't the war everywhere? The Italian, German and the French troops were marching without stopping on the main road very close by. One does not ask who is a friend or an enemy. At the slightest alert, the inhabitants of Bourg take refuge behind the thick walls of the Gonzaguina, the castle where Jean lives. Children listen to the adults repeat tales of atrocities, extortions, plundering, rapes and massacres. Out of this daily tragedy, they have made a game. Very naturally, because he is the biggest in size, Jean is the chief. His army, composed of a dozen barefoot peasant boys, fight incessantly against an enemy who is omnipresent but always invisible.

While, superficially speaking, nothing amongst these children could distinguish one from the other, whether in their behaviour, their vocabulary or their body language, an observer could, however, remark that Jean was different from the others, beginning with the clothes. Though his doublet and his boots are well worn-out, patched, covered in stains, the other kids are content in rags. While the latter were free with their time while their parents worked in the fields, Jean was never without surveillance even for a minute. Even at playtime, two people watched over him from a distance. Dona Carmela was his nanny before she became his governess. She was a big girl, solid, powerfully built, with a carnivorous laugh, a crude vocabulary and a weakness for wine. Generous, open, she kept aside all her affection, all her love, for Jean. Father Soragno was a more complicated personality. Moreover, this Dominican took liberties with his Order. He invented a half-religious half-civilian attire for himself. The doublet and the lord's knee breeches were accompanied by the white cloak of a monk. His deviances were obviously approved by the higher authorities, which only proved that the good father held a certain power. He was always game for a laugh with his jokes. He had a thundering laugh, a warrior's build, and honoured the pleasures of eating. He had a piercing gaze and his expression could become severe. Even though he spoke often in a loud voice, he remained immensely prudent, discreet, and reserved. He seemed frank, but one could never tell what was on his mind.

As far as his memory served, Jean had never known of any place other than Gonzaguina. A century before, the marquises of Mantoue had built this fortress at the frontiers of their territory which was constantly attacked since their small state in the north of Italy occupied a strategic position. Also their neighbours, important Italian principalities and republics behaved like powerful foreigners who had but one idea: to subjugate them. Moreover, the rules of strategy had evolved, Gonzaguina was more or less abandoned in exchange for the newer defense systems. It still belonged to the present Marquis of Mantoue, Alphonse, to whom it recalled the patronymic name. Gonzaguina, in fact, is the diminutive of Gonzague, the name of the dynasty that ruled Mantoue. The farmers of the marquis had little by little occupied it, but in spite of this peaceful transformation, its walls were still in good condition and even now knew how to resist assaults. Jean, with his mentors, Dona Carmela and Father Soragno, occupied the old apartments of the governor of the fortress, with large rooms, rather dilapidated, yet habitable where crude furniture made by the carpenters of the estate stood next to debris of the glory of former times.

The landscape around was sadly flat. Fields spread out to the horizon, sometimes fenced by thin trees. The river wound between the high artificial banks meant to prevent it from overflowing, the flat top of which served as a promenade for the peasants. Though close to one of the principal main north-to-south roads of Italy, Gonzaguina remained isolated. Almost no one stopped there. On the other hand, its inhabitants had only a few leagues to cover to get news in the big villages bordering the highway.

For Dona Carmela, Jean was the child she never had. Devoid of sentimentality and silliness, she enwrapped him with a maternal love which was warm and bracing, but could the governess alone replace a father, a mother, brothers, sisters, cousins and grandparents? Jean was alone in this world. He knew it, he felt it, and he lived it.

Father Soragno took care that Jean mixed with other children of the village and paid attention to the fact that there be no difference in the treatment towards him. But on the other hand, he differentiated him in educating him. Jean was the only child in Gonzaguina who learnt how to read and write.

He led the normal life of a six-year-old child in the isolated village in the north of Italy, and yet his presence there was not very normal. The peasants only knew that he was under the orders and under the protection of their ruler, the Marquis of Mantoue. Instinctively, they sensed a secret around his existence. His playmates, also, in their unintentional attitude, showed that they felt he was different from them, sometimes by the marks of respect that slipped out of them, sometimes by harder blows, an unconscious revenge against the master. Smaller than him in size, his tormenters were more muscular than him. With his too thin and too long hands, he defended himself valiantly. At times, he would be below them, but he never asked for their mercy, and he waited to be alone to cry over his humiliation.

In the year 1527, spring was late, and had only just begun in mid-April. The timid arrival of pleasant times was nevertheless enough to put the children in a state of excitement. They thought only of playing, they became untamable, and constantly disappeared into the wilderness.

As for the peasants, they grumbled constantly because the flowers in the fields, exceptionally lush, choked their wheat, because the birds – larger in number than ever before – stole their grain, because war had again resumed. Troops marched afresh through the marquisate of Mantoue. This time around, the French, the Germans, under the command of the Commander of Bourbon, marched towards Rome, on the orders of the Emperor Charles Quint. Subtly warmed up by their priest, the inhabitants of the region were outraged. How did the Emperor, who was also the very catholic king of Spain, who had led a war without mercy against the heretical Protestants, dare attack the Pope?

Was he worse than the schismatics, the Moors and the Saracens? And what could be said of his loyal lieutenant, the Commander, a traitor who had lost all his scruples and decency!

The peasants hated these soldiers who went singing towards Rome. However, these ones conducted themselves far better than the other soldiers that they had seen march through their lands in the past. Fifty thousand men of the Commander were far too many in number to take anything but the highway. All the routes of the region saw them pass, even the one that made a large detour by Gonzaguina.

On the arrival of the first soldiers, the peasants quickly took refuge in the fortress, the doors of which they barricaded. Then they noticed that the intruders kept a certain discipline and robbed far less than their predecessors. They also noticed that the German mercenaries were worse than the Gascons. Meanwhile, soon after, they returned to their fields, which were in need of their hands. They worked normally at the same time staying on alert, ready, at the slightest hitch, to run to the shelter of the fortress.

The chickens and the goats disappeared everyday. The soldiers were a bit too persistent in asking them for food and drink, but no major incident had taken place, which did not prevent the peasants from complaining, from moaning non-stop.

Father Soragno kept himself well updated on the entire situation and even more so on the criticism regarding the Emperor and the

Commander. He maintained his temperament and gave, as was customary, writing lessons to Jean.

One day, a coach arrived in Gonzaguina carrying a letter for Father Soragno. After reading the letter, very calmly he asked a servant to saddle a horse and asked Dona Carmela to pack a few things of Jean, for they both would be gone a few days. When they were ready, he helped Jean climb the croup and both of them set out towards the north. They rejoined the main road where they struggled to make their way through much traffic: entire regiments coming in the opposite direction, carriages, horses heading towards Milan. They stayed two nights in packed inns where they needed all the authority and a bit of Father Soragno's gold to find beds. On approaching the Lombardy capital, they traversed huge military encampments of the Commander of Bourbon's armies, now more than half deserted. Jean was stunned by so much movement, such noise, and so many human beings. With much amazement, he surveyed the crowd, the buildings and the shops. They reached a palace that seemed enormous to a small boy, guarded by a large number of guards. Father Soragno gave his name and they were allowed to pass. They climbed a large marble staircase, and passed through numerous rooms full of functionaries, military men, courtiers. Jean had his eyes fixed on the ceiling, fascinated by the frescos depicting all the mythological gods. He was so distracted by what he saw that he stumbled onto a number of important personalities.

They arrived in front of a firmly shut door, guarded by yeomen, arms at the ready. Again, Father Soragno presented his name to a secretary and they were not made to wait for long. They entered a room only a little smaller than the previous ones but more richly adorned with marble, bronze, and frescos. A number of military men in their armour surrounded a man a lot bigger than the rest around a table covered with military cards. His black armour, the only one encrusted with gold, sparkled. There was complete silence as the monk and the child approached him. Jean was surprised to discover in his tutor a humble, almost servile attitude towards the master in black and gold. Father Soragno very softly pushed Jean towards him. The child noticed that his beard was as dark as his curly hair, his nose hooked, his eyes dark and piercing. These were fixed on Jean with such intensity that they seemed to want to pierce through him. Jean recoiled within, but at the same time he knew that there was nothing to be afraid of the lord. Instead of lowering his eyes, he fixed them on him. The gazes of the child and of the imposing knight met for a long moment. Seized by a deep emotion, the knight pulled himself together, and with an imperious gesture with his metal-gloved hand, he approached Father Soragno. He leaned towards him and exchanged a few sentences that no one could hear. He then held out a little object to Jean that he clasped in his hands. Then with a gesture, he dismissed them. After they had left, Jean pulled at Father Soragno's sleeve, 'Who is he?'

'He is a hero,' the monk responded mysteriously.

Jean contemplated the object given to him by the knight. This bag of powder contained the explosives that the knights used for their firearms. Its dark skin was so used that it had almost become black. On the reverse, it bore a crudely enameled badge. 'These are the arms of the dukes of Bourbon, a field of *fleur de lys* crossed by a red bar,' Father Soragno told him. While observing the coat of arms fixed on the bag, he had become pensive. Jean, who had always known him to be vigilant, mind on alert and never short of words, was surprised to see him lost in extraordinary speculations.

They immediately took the road to return home. On arriving in Gonzaguina, Father Soragno convened the peasants, 'Listen, listen, his lordship the Commander of Bourbon had called me to Milan to tell me that he has given very strict orders that his troops not touch your fields and not come close to Gonzaguina.' Shaking their heads and still grumbling, the peasants dispersed.

Soon the stream of the Commander's troops dried up and calm returned to the region. The peasants were particularly occupied with their fields that season and did not leave the territory. They didn't go in search of news and news didn't not come to Gonzaguina, which lived thus for several weeks, cut off from the world.

One evening, at the end of May, when Jean, along with Dona Carmela and Father Soragno, was finishing his frugal dinner in the main hall that also served as the classroom, they heard vigorous knocking on the door of the fortress. Soon they faced a man, tall, lanky, frighteningly thin, and heavily moustached, with blazing eyes under thick salt-and-pepper eyebrows. He introduced himself as the Sergeant of Aurigni, a loyal companion of his lordship the Commander of Bourbon in all his campaigns. The Commander had sent him to Gonzaguina. Father Soragno eagerly asked him the latest news. In a husky voice and as if spitting out his words, the sergeant announced that Rome had fallen into the hands of the Commander's troops. Unfortunately, the Pope managed to escape the punishment that awaited him. He had shut himself in the Saint-Ange castle and was holding out the attackers. 'But,' added the sergent, 'we well avenged the Pope Clement, his Rome, and we put it in a real nice state.'

Seeing the interest of his alighted listeners and without taking into account Jean's tender age, he eloquently launched into a recital of the sack of the eternal city. 'We set big palaces on fire, we burnt all the churches that we found on our way, but before that we took out all that seemed precious to us, the jewels, the crystals, brocades, ivory-inlayed furniture, golden ewers, silver altars. We looted a bit, but above all, we threw all of that in the middle of the road, we trampled on their treasures, we made our horses go over it so as to crush it a bit better. The relics – which seemed were the most precious in Christianity – we kept them for gambling while we drank in the evenings around the campfire set up in places. The cardinals were tried, as we succeeded in catching quite a few who didn't have the time to catch up with their patron saint in the Saint-Ange castle. We didn't kill them, we only satisfied ourselves with manhandling them. So they arrived in front of our tribunals in tattered red cloaks and many bruises. We terrorized them, making them believe that we were going to execute them. In fact, after a few well-salted jokes, we sent them back to the devil, their master, for these big cats knew nothing! On the contrary, we tortured the priests so that they would reveal the hiding place of their treasures; these nasty animals had hidden a lot before we reached their churches. Each one of us came up with a torture worse than the other, and they yelled, these good fellows, they screamed breaking our eardrums! As for the nuns, the wives, the mothers, the daughters, we raped each one who we found on our way, even the old, even the ugly, even the really young. They didn't scream as much as the priests, they squealed, they wailed, and we, we laughed. We then headed towards Saint-Pierre. Everywhere the dying ones asked us to finish them, end their misery, we kicked them with our feet and left them to their well-deserved fate. In front of the Basilica, we saw in the middle a sort of a strange column, it seemed it was called an obelisk. We had fun making it the target and pierced it with bullets. A good number of Swiss guards continued to fight. We continued to kill till the very last one. Moreover, not even one asked for mercy. Inside the basilica, along with the priests, there were still the monks, who defended themselves like lions. We massacred them all and very carefully piled their corpses on the main-altar. Then, we got our horses inside the basilica and we transformed it into a stable and toilets.'

Jean did not understand all that he heard, but enough to understand that it was about things so horrific as to be inconceivable. The monk and the governess were petrified with horror. The sergeant, happy with the attention of his audience, continued for a long time and probably added even more. Finally, Dona Carmela managed to utter: 'But why all this monstrosity?'

'Well, of course, to avenge the Commander's death.'

'He is dead!' cried Dona Carmela and the monk.

'How come, didn't you know that? He was killed in the very first assault. As always, he was the first to attack. He had climbed the first step with his sword in his fist on the ladder put up against the walls of Rome, but very soon, he was shot in his side by a musket. He fell. We brought him under a tree. The wound was fatal, he did not delay in surrendering his soul. In the meantime, his troops, following the tactic that he had himself put to practice, had taken Rome. Living, he could not conquer the eternal city, but dead he had. Also, we organized a triumphed entry for him. We pulled down a section of the walls of Rome, and he entered, preceded and followed by his army, spread out on a stretcher, eyes still open to be able to witness his triumph. We took him till the Vatican in what they call the

Sistine chapel, we lay him down on a golden sheet and his entire army marched in front of him.'

Jean felt a strange emotion come over him. He had met the Commander for only a few moments and the latter had been content to just look at him without saying a word. And yet, an indefinable sentiment seized him. The grief was mixed with the conviction of having lost his only support. He took out from his pocket the skin of gunpowder with the crest of the Bourbons and clenched it tight with all his strength in his hand. Dona Carmela cried hot tears. She recounted how she knew the Commander as a child, 'His mother brought me with her to France when she married his father, she was so beautiful, so nice, our Clara di Gonzagua.' Then, proud of her acquaintances, she added, aiming at the sergeant, 'She belonged to the reigning family of Mantoue, she was the aunt of the present marquis, Alphonse, our king.' Father Soragno remained sullen, less out of emotion than practicality. 'The Commander is dead and we are left with no money, for it was him who provided for us.'

'On the contrary, my father,' intervened the Sergeant of Aurigni, 'I bring you tidings. The day before the assault on Rome, the Commander had called for me. He entrusted me a war treasure destined for the education of your pupil Jean,' and he heavily put down on the table a big sack out of which one heard the fine tinkling sound of coins. Father Soragno could not stop himself from opening it. It contained gold doubloons by the thousands. 'The Commander also ordered me to stay close to you so I can protect you if the need arises, and later to make a soldier out of Jean. Father Soragno winced, and Dona Carmela's heart almost jumped out of her mouth at the thought of this brute who had happily participated in the atrocities during the pillaging of Rome, becoming Jean's military trainer. But how was one to chase away this faithful of the Commander?

The years went by. The Emperor and the Pope reconciled. The King of France, disillusioned by his failures in the peninsula, closed the chapter of wars with Italy. On the other hand, his rivalry with the Emperor continued in bursts of wars, of treaties, of changing of alliances and dramatic resurgences. Even though the Italian States continued every now and then to indulge in squabbles, peace of a kind had returned to Italy, which spread up to this isolated corner of the Marquis of Mantoue called Gonzaguina. Jean grew up, Dona Carmela aged, and Father Soragno, who was lettered, very lettered in fact, now taught his pupil the subjects in which he excelled: history, geography, mathematics; literature and poetry he ignored, and theology was far from being his forte. Jean was enwrapped in stories of wars, of battles and the important events of the past centuries.

Whenever his warrior dreams carried him away, Jean looked at the Commander's skin of gunpowder that was always with him. This object reminded him of the one who gave it to him, who had become in his mind the most magnificent hero in history, and the role model he wanted to live up to.

Jean stayed true to his blood. He was born to be a soldier and the Sergeant of Aurigni helped him understand that. The brute had developed affection for the young boy. 'He reminds me of the Commander,' he would say, 'and yet there is no link between them.' He had become an attentive and competent military trainer. After having taught him the basics of war, he trained him in his favourite field, artillery. He had always served in the artillery; he loved cannons like he loved his fiancées, and knew how to transmit this sentiment to Jean. In Gonzaguina there existed only two old ruined cannons. He compensated for that by getting the local carpenter to make the most modern wooden artillery models of the day. He observed with joy that Jean learnt fast and became more and more passionate about his beloved cannons.

Jean's status remained both exceptional and veiled in mystery. He was a full member of the miniscule community of Gonzaguina. When, by chance, a traveller, a foreigner or a trader adventured up to the old fortress, Father Soragno always took care that Jean was not seen. Without forcing him, he succeeded in isolating him from the intruder. Jean never left Gonzaguina and his acquaintances from the big world were limited to those of whom he learnt about from the father and the sergeant. At the end of adolescence, he was close to considering Gonzaguina a prison and dreamt of discovering the horizons. In 1539, he turned eighteen years old.

Jean continued to sleep in the same room as Father Soragno. One dark and deep night in the thick of winter, they both awoke with a start hearing cries and an uproar. 'Kill, kill!' screamed the hoarse voices. They heard the noise of windowpanes being smashed, doors being broken down, of heavy steps running in the galleries. They heard painful yells, agonized wailings, they recognized the voice of Dona Carmela, 'Hel...' she didn't have the time to finish her call for help.

Jean leaped for his sword and Father Soragno did the same, for the good monk had taken his precautions and always kept a weapon close to him. The Sergeant of Aurigni rushed into the room, his heavy double-edged sword in his hand. The assassins, twelve to fifteen of them followed him and a ferocious battle began. Jean had for himself the force and the energy of his youth, but also the inexperience. He was going to receive a fatal blow when the sergeant of Aurigni threw himself in front of him and received across his chest a cut from the sword meant for Jean. Father Soragno defended himself like a professional fighter. He must have become a monk very late in life because it was evident from the way he used his arms that he had spent many years in the army. Though they had knocked down several of their assailants, it was evident that they were not going to hold for very long. 'Ayuto!, help,' screamed Father Soragno. The peasants had not waited for the plea for help. They had already awakened and heard the agonized screams of the servants and of Dona Carmela. They knew the killers would not spare them, for there would be no witness to this sort of crime. Carrying torches, armed with their scythes and pitchforks, they flooded the courtyard of the fortress and climbed the stairs with great speed to defend Jean and the father. The attackers caught sight of them. There was a moment of hesitation. Then, one distinctively heard, coming from the outside, a piercing whistle followed by a single word, an order. The attackers immediately ran away. They ran over the walls, climbing down the ladders that they had put for invading the fortress and disappeared into the darkness of the night.

The attack didn't last for more than a quarter of an hour. A counting of the dead was done: Dona Carmela didn't have to suffer for her throat had been slit. The Sergeant of Aurigni had carried out the orders of his master, the deceased Commander – he had protected Jean at the cost of his own life. Not a single servant had survived. Six of the attackers were killed. Father Soragno examined them for a long time. 'Professionals, Italian, but they are not from here. Jean, did you hear the order that their invisible chief gave which made them flee?' Jean had not understood the word, he had only heard a sort of a yelp, without understanding the meaning. Father Soragno said with a pensive air, 'I am almost sure I heard the word "retreat" in French. Their chief was thus French.'

'But who? Why? What did he want? Who did he want to kill?' asked Jean.

'There is no time to find this out,' replied Soragno, 'we must leave immediately for they will return in force, these people will not get their reward without having finished their task, which is to kill us.' Despite the pleas of Jean in tears, Father Soragno did not allow him to attend the funeral of Dona Carmela, of Aurigni, and of the others. 'We don't have the time,' he repeated.

The sun had not yet risen when they left Gonzaguina. In a few days they had reached the republic of Genoa and found passage on a Spanish merchant ship that was going to Carthage.

'Why Spain?' asked Jean who, until now, had docilely followed Father Soragno without posing any questions.

'Because the Emperor who is also the king of Spain is the most fierce adversary of King François.'

Jean had to content himself with this explanation, of which he understood nothing.

In this wintry season, the winds were strong and pushed the ship along rapidly. It was cold but beautiful over the Mediterranean. The sun shone during the day and at night all the stars were out. One evening, Jean and Father Soragno stayed on the deck, wrapped in their houppelandes to resist the temperature, incapable of detaching themselves from the splendid spectacle of the starry night. Without the need of saying it, they knew that the moment for a conclusive talk had arrived.

Jean began, 'Who am I?'

'I know you have asked yourself this question incessantly for years now about your identity. The only reason I could not talk to you about it is that I don't know who you are. I only know that a deep mystery surrounds your birth.'

This irritated Jean. 'Even so there have to be some clues! Someone must know. Maybe you know more than you are saying.'

Father Soragno calmed him down, 'Allow me first to tell you my story. I am, as you know, a native of Mantoue. I came to France in the train of Clara de Gonzague when she married the Commander's father, and I was introduced to the opulent court of the dukes of Bourbon. When Clara died, her son, the Commander, asked me to stay close to him. Hence I passed many years in the Moulins Castle. One day, it was in 1521, the Commander called for me. I was a bit surprised by the late and unusual hour of this summoning. I found him alone in his studio, which had been copied from the style of the Italian princes. He held out a sort of a basket to me that looked like it was full of linen. At the bottom there was a newborn, a boy, you, Jean. The Commander offered me no explanation about the origin of this child, but he gave me precise instructions: I had to take him under my charge, on the same night, to Italy, to the marquisate of Mantoue. The Commander had everything ready, the escort who was to accompany me, the money that was going to be necessary and letters meant for the Marquis of Mantoue, his first cousin. I carried the newly born, arrived in Mantoue, introduced myself to the monarch and handed over the letters from the Commander. Immediately after having read them, he gave orders. This is how I came to Gonzaguina where everything was prepared to receive us. Dona Carmela was appointed to assist me, for she had also come to France with Princess Clara, but at the latter's death, she was sent back to her native city Mantoue. Both of us were appointed the task of raising you, and the Commander insistently advised me to make sure that no one knew of your existence. He said this to me with the frightening air that this fierce man was known to take and it made me tremble. Now I told myself that the only way to hide you was not by locking you up but by letting you mix with the children of the village. My method was successful because, for eighteen years, no one discovered your existence nor came to bother us.'

Lost in his thoughts, Jean was no longer listening to Father Soragno whom he interrupted, 'So, that makes me the Commander's son....'

'You may be the illegitimate son of some great lord, of some honourable lady, of relatives or friends of the Commander, whom he wanted to help, by hiding an embarrassing birth and by taking responsibility for the future of the child. This happens a lot in the most illustrious families. Often, in order to hide a bastard, another dynasty shoulders the responsibility.'

'Do you know, my father, what I have suffered these past years during which I have slowly become conscious of the mystery that surrounds me? I was one amongst the others, and yet I was different. I have caught people's looks, whispers of the village women, the allusions that the men have allowed themselves while sniggering "Who is he?" Who am I? I need an identity. Thus, rather than an unknown father, a mother lost in the mist, I'd prefer to believe that I am the bastard of the Commander and from now on these arms that adorn this bag of gunpowder are mine.'

'If what you're saying is right, I don't see why he had to hide your existence to this extent, when he raised in the eyes and knowledge of the world a little bastard that he had before his marriage with a French woman whose name I have forgotten. What is more, in the illustrious families, bastards, far from being hidden, were flaunted visibly almost with pride.'

'I have learnt to know you, father, mysteries irritate you, obscurity annoys you, ... you have to have clarity, and you certainly have created a key to the mystery of my identity.'

The monk smiled, amused at having been unveiled by the young adolescent.

'I did indeed came up with a hypothesis, so unbelievable that it took me time to accept it. You could very simply be the legitimate son of the Commander and his wife the Duchess Suzanne. But why then would they have hidden your birth? Suzanne, it was known to all, could not have any more children, you then would have been the only heir to her enormous fortune, a fortune that for so many years the mother of the King François, Madam Louise, lusted after. Now, she had already proved that, once her cupidity or her ambition lit up, nothing stopped her. The Commander and the Duchess Suzanne must have been convinced that she would inevitably succeed in wiping out their child. The only way to protect him thus was to conceal his birth and to raise him away from France, as the biggest secret, till the clouds cleared up, in other words, till Louise went to hell where she was impatiently awaited.

'When the Commander entrusted you to me, Duchess Suzanne had just delivered without anyone in the castle as yet aware about the sex of the child or about the state of its health. When I arrived in Mantoue, I learnt that she had given birth to a dead son, as the Commander had officially announced. Who would have known that this announcement was simply a charade to hide the truth? This truth being that the Duchess had not only given birth to a child who was very much alive, but also that he was immediately removed from Moulins. Meanwhile, allies were required to help with the situation. Thus, the Commander and probably his wife Suzanne requested help from their cousin, the Marquis of Mantoue. They entrusted you to two natives from Mantoue, who had known and loved Princess Clara a lot. All his life, and even after his death, the Commander very generously looked after you through the Sergeant of Aurigni. This evidence of your identity is not enough. Another evidence that I consider more significant is our brief meeting with the Commander when he was getting ready to march on Rome and the gift that he gave you, a valueless bag of gunpowder but with his crest. With his crest! Do you understand Jean, what that means?'

'You therefore believe that I am the legitimate son of the Commander.'

Father Soragno took a long time to think before he responded, 'I indeed believe that, but I have no proof.'

'Do I resemble my parents?'

'You get your dark hair and your complexion from the Commander whereas your almond-shaped blue eyes come from the duchess, but one must not give too much importance to resemblances.'

'Have you imagined, what the Commander's intentions could have been concerning my future?'

'Maybe he had hoped, that after capturing Rome, and if all went well, to have you to come close to him. Madam Louise, the King's mother, no longer posed any danger. Declared a traitor to France, and of the King, he was in no position to claim his inheritance on which, moreover, she had already got her hands. He could thus, without any risk, make your existence known. But he is dead. I did not move. Eight years later, Madam Louise died. I still did not budge, even though her death erased the threat that weighed on you. However, I preferred to hold on to the Commander's instructions and continue to raise you as the biggest possible secret. The unexpected and brutal attack we were the victims of proved to me that I wasn't wrong in doing so. I was not all the same completely mistaken, I heard the chief of the assassins give the retreat order in French. Thus, if their chief was French, we can suppose that their backers were French. They were not bandits or looters, those men who failed to take our lives, they were assassins paid to kill. To kill who? A few peasants, a monk, an old lady, a retired sergeant? Of course not. It was you they had come to kill. Which proves that Madam Louise's death did not erase the threat weighing over you. Why does anyone want to finish you? Who wishes that? Perhaps, quite simply the heir of Madam Louise, King François. Think about it, if it were proven that a legitimate son of the Commander existed, the King of France would have had to return to him an enormous fortune of which, at present, he is taking advantage. But even there, I am only limited to speculations, I do not have any proofs.'

'And now, what is going to become of us, what am I going to do?'

'You have turned eighteen years old, it is up to you to decide.'

'I am tempted to go to France to find out the truth about my birth and to reclaim my inheritance. As the Commander's son, I could be one of the primary lords of Europe. At present, I am nothing.'

'Yes, you are.'

And Father Soragno counted the number of qualities that he found in his pupil. The pretty flat reply failed to lighten up Jean's spirits. He wanted to have some time until they reached Spain to contemplate a manner in which he could take his destiny in his hands. He had no time for leisure.

Egypt 1539

The day after this conversation, the ship sailed in the middle of the morning, pushed along by a rather strong wind. The weather was magnificent; it was almost hot. Suddenly, the ship's guard let out an alarmed cry. The captain adjusted his telescope, then, horrified by what he saw, simply let drop the word 'Barbarians'. Soon after, Jean, Father Soragno and the passengers, most of them rich merchants, could make out in the distance a sail that grew bigger rapidly. It was the barbaric pirates, the terror of the Mediterranean. The enemy ship was getting inexorably closer. The captain tried to reassure everyone: his ship was ready for all eventualities, had a large crew that was well armed, they had all it took to fight off the pirates. The latter would have known that one did not attack a Spanish ship with impunity! To Father Soragno who stood on his sides, he murmured an all-together different version, 'The barbarians,' he whispered so that no one overheard, 'are spies in all the ports of the Mediterranean. They know where we are coming from, what we are carrying, and which direction we will take. They have been waiting for us. We will not be able to hold against them, we have no hope.' The rich merchants did not hear this observation, but Jean did not miss a single word. So he made up his mind that their victory would be dearly bought. The sailors of the crew, who knew these barbarians, shared the pessimism of the captain. Jean sensed a clear-cut doubt amongst them.

The enemy ship was only a few cable lengths away and the way they were equipped was not meant to put anyone at ease. Their gaudy clothes, their swords that they waved in the air, their formidable moustaches, their terrifying faces, and the howls they produced could undermine the most courageous morale. This, moreover, was part of a deliberate tactic. They threw their ropes, jumped over the deck and attacked the sailors. The latter defended themselves limply. A few wounded, one or two dead, and they immediately surrendered. Cut off on the back deck, Father Soragno, the captain and Jean, protecting the merchants pressed together behind them, fought valiantly. Father Soragno cried out to his pupil, 'The captain and me, we have nothing to lose, but you, you surrender immediately, you might have a chance.' The only response Jean gave was to continue to fight with an increased fervour. However, the pirates who were all well armed, surrounded the three men as well as the prisoners. There wasn't any need to ask the merchants for their arms, they had not for a minute thought of defending themselves, and they knew they were going to be spared...

All resistance crushed, turmoil ceased and the methodical side of the barbaric pirates was victorious. They started to transport onto their ship all the merchandise, all objects, all goods, and everything in general that could be of use on the merchant ship. They behaved with great order and without haste, visibly involved in their task. They then took care of the prisoners, and started to sort them out. First were the potential slaves, which meant young and therefore strong men, almost all the sailors and Jean. Next were the 'ransoms', in other words, the rich merchants. These would be carried in captivity, more or less well treated, and after a certain time, if their ransom did not arrive, they would very simply be beheaded. But everyone could and wanted to pay, and this the pirates knew. And finally, the 'useless', which meant men who were too old to be sold as slaves or too poor to pay a ransom, which meant a few sailors, Father Soragno and the captain. They began with the sailors, dragging them without pity despite their pleas and flung them off board. The captain, with lips sealed and no pleas, died with dignity. Now they took Father Soragno when Jean intervened. He cried out in Italian, the language in which he had heard the captain of the pirates jabber in, 'Father is in service of the King of France for many years now. The latter will never pardon you for killing him. I myself am a subject of the King of France. You will regret it if you touch a single strand of our hair.' The pirate exploded in thundering laughter, and in an Italian-Hispanic-Arabian pidgin which Jean did succeed in understanding, he belched out his words, 'Don't you know, you jackanapes, that if we are here, it is not only with the permission but also on the express command of the King of France, who has made an alliance with the shadow of Allah on earth, the Badshah[1] Suleiman? The King of France begged our master Barbarousse, sovereign of Algeria, lieutenant of the Badshah, to send his invincible fighters to attack all ships bearing the flag of the King of Spain. Frenchman, you will be sold a slave with the blessings of the King of France!' and while laughing he mimicked the blessing of a Christian priest. Rage provided Jean with new force. In one movement, he freed himself from the pirates who were holding him, grabbed a sword from one of them and threw himself on their captain. Another pirate was faster, and with the hilt of his sword he gave Jean such a strong blow that he instantly fell unconscious. It was in this state that he was moved to the pirate ship along with the other prisoners. Father Soragno ended his life, by jumping into the sea rather than being pushed by the pirates. The pirates set the merchant ship on fire and it sank gently into the Mediterranean.

Jean found himself at the bottom of the ship's hold, chained along with the other sailors destined for slavery. For others it was hopelessness, for him it was humiliation. This vast ship's hold was full of human misery. Jean thought of Father Soragno all the time. After his disappearance, Jean found himself with an increased sense of solitude that had been with him since his birth. No one alive to think of, no one alive to love, no one alive to help him. But as he heard the other sailors moan with the thought of never seeing their parents, their wives, their children, he told himself that perhaps he was better off than others. Dwelling over the happenings of his short life, he wondered if he was born under an unlucky star, and if the rest of his remaining life would continue to be marked by misfortune. A slave was what he was destined to be till his death... for a slave never escapes.

And yet, from time to time, a bizarre conviction would come to him from somewhere deep inside that not everything was as dark as it seemed. He had confidence in himself and in some corner of his conscience, he refused to admit that his existence was to be limited to slavery. The treatment that he suffered along with his unfortunate companions whittled away at this wisp of optimism. In the stifling ship hold, where they were cramped against each other, they could hardly breathe. The prison guards threw them just enough food to keep them from starvation. Their aim was to break down as fast as possible the will of these men. They hit them at random with their clubs, they whipped them at the slightest murmur of protest, they shouted from morning till evening.

Weakened, terrified, the men were soon made incapable of sitting up and reacting. Sensing that Jean was different from the others and was more headstrong, the thugs concentrated on him. His body turned black and blue and was covered with bloody bruises left by the whip. The guards, who knew how to inflict the worst possible suffering, took care that they did not damage the merchandise too much. At the end of ten days of sailing, when they reached Alexandria, Jean felt all his resistance of will melt away.

Upon disembarking, the Egyptian bureaucracy was waiting for them, for they were being passed on from the hands of the pirate captain to those of the slave traders. Their employers sat behind desks piled with fat registers, evaluating each piece. They examined the health, the characteristics of the slaves one by one, and noted the results of their evaluation: height, weight, state of the teeth, age, strength, and signs of illness. For each one, the buyer fixed a price. The chief pirate had had enough to pull his hair out. The haggling went on for a long time during which the slaves were waiting under the glaring sun. Then began the drama – for in reality it felt almost like a play, always the same one, played out by the same actors, who were also always the same – so when the play came to an end, the sum total was counted to the chief pirate and the merchant took his purchases onto a felucca. The sailors raised the sails and the ship began to go up the Nile. It was not a ship that floated deep in the water; it had no hold so as to avoid the sand banks. The slaves were chained on the deck. The merciless Egyptian sun beat down on them from dawn till dusk, their skin reddened, cracked, their body burnt, moaned for one drop of water which the guards refused them. Jean had only one thought in his mind: to keep his senses. He saw enticing banks unfold before him where green fields spread out watered by an excellent system of canals alternating with palm groves. He thought about the peaceful and active life of the peasants of the village. He envied this modest happiness that he would never know.

It took them several days to reach Boulaq, the port of Cairo. In the past, the city had spread out far from the banks of Nile, but it had since spilled over its medieval walls and little by little eaten up the rich orchards that lay between her and the river. Now Boulaq and Cairo were part of one city.

Once the felucca was docked, the slaves descended and chained to one another took the route called Boulaq under the supervision of the merchant and his assistants. Exhaustion had made them almost incapable of moving forward and the prison guards whipped them with a heightened cruelty as they approached their destination. In this state they went by the suburbs where some orchards still survived.

They crossed the city walls of Cairo by the Bab Futua gate. Bloodless, haggard, Jean felt completely dazed by the noise, the movements, the smell, the colours that surrounded them on all sides. Milan, which he had visited once in his childhood, seemed like a village in comparison. He had never imagined that there could ever be a city so big and so populated. They couldn't help slowing down their steps despite the summons of their merchant; they managed with great difficulty to move forward in the middle of the dense crowd. He felt damaged, demeaned, forced to march in rags, semi-nude, chained like a criminal, whipped as if a beast of burden, but no one paid attention to the slaves.

Thus they arrived at a caravanserai meant exclusively for slaves. They came from all corners of the world, locked in huge hangars which bordered three sides of a big courtyard in the middle of which lay the offices of the merchants. The slaves remained chained in groups. Jean was part of one with the sailors from the Spanish ship. They were left to stagnate for many days in their filth and misery. Some of the slaves fell ill, their guards were immediately warned to take them away no one knew where – in any case they never reappeared again. Silence of the deepest kind reigned in the sheds for they were prohibited from uttering the least word. Everyone waited for that day in the week devoted to the selling of slaves.

The day before, Jean and the sailors were untied and sent to clean themselves in the hamam of the shelter. They received new clothes and a double portion of food. As the sale approached, they polished their merchandise. Apprehension clutched the heart of Jean and his companions. He wondered what the narrow universe in which he was to be closed for the rest of his remaining days looked like. However, in spite of all that he had suffered at the hands of the slave-guards, he perceived at the end of the tunnel, far away, a tiny ray of light.

Early next morning, the prison guards jerked them awake. Cleaned, dressed, fed, they were made to line up in the courtyard of the shelter with slaves from other lots. The merchants appeared nervous. The slaves understood that they awaited an important visit. They learnt from the whispers of their guards that Omer Bey, one of the six assistants of the Viceroy of Egypt, inspector of the army, and thus the chief recruiter was visiting them. His position gave him the right to inspect the slaves before they were put to auction. He thus had first choice to fill up his army ranks. A hubbub told Jean that the important person had arrived.

Surrounded by an assembly of military men and officials, Omer Bey approached. A roly-poly figure with a goatee and searching eyes, he wore a white djellaba and an abaya embroidered with gold, with a tall green turban as headgear. From all the batches in front of him for his inspection, he had chosen only three robust toughies; Jean's lot was the last. He barely looked at the unfortunate sailor companions of Jean's, who if not booked by the army inspector were to be sold on auction a bit later. He stopped for a long time in front of Jean. He was facing a big good-looking boy, powerful yet gracefully built, with elongated blue eyes, hair that was almost black, a pleasant expression and a look that pierced through. In the Italianized gibberish that seemed like the international language of the Mediterranean, he asked him where he was from. Jean explained he was raised on a farm in the north of Italy. 'There is nothing of a peasant about you.'

Jean replied, 'I never got to know my parents, they died at my birth.'

'In any case, your appearance does not lie, you are undoubtedly a descendant of a very grand family.'

Then, Omer Bey turned towards one of his lieutenants and barked some orders in a language that Jean understood to be Turkish. Two guards grabbed him and took him away. They passed through Cairo to arrive at the bottom of the impressive citadel that dominated the city, built by the fabulous Saladin on a spur of a rock at the edge of the desert. Jean, surrounded by the guards, climbed the ramp, passed under the imposing bastion of the entrance and entered a mini-city: the citadel comprised palaces one of which included that of the viceroy, Dawood Pasha; mosques, hamams, administrative buildings, gardens, arms shops, warehouses where stocks of wheat were stored against famines, and finally several barracks. It was to one of these that Jean was taken.

From the next day, his training began. He was put under such an intense routine that he didn't even have the time to think. Waking up at dawn along with other young recruits who shared his dormitory, he barely had the time to get ready. The whole day was devoted to exercising.

In the evenings he was so tired that he would collapse on his bed. The trainers were not cruel but demanding and severe. They were not unfair, but they punished on the smallest of mistakes. A second of inattention got them their punishment. This regime, while taking all of Jean's time and extracting all his strength until complete exhaustion, prevented the temptation of despair. But he had the impression of having lost his personality, his identity.

At the end of one year's training, he was judged ready to be sent to the front. Egypt bled from endemic conflicts, the war with Yemen, a province in perpetual disorder, and Bedouin tribal revolts. Jean did not feel any hatred towards these enemies of the Egyptian regime. He was more sympathetic to their cause of liberty. However, from the first involvement, he understood that it was going to be him or them. They were not going to give any quarter, and to survive, he had to defend himself... and kill. His atavism spoke up as well. He enjoyed battling enemies who were dangerous, valorous and indomitable.

It was not long before his superiors noticed his qualities. To begin with, Jean showed a surprising resistance to the pitiless heat of the desert, to physical fatigue, to danger. What's more, he knew how to take initiative when he had to. He was revealed to be a born chief. His men idolized him and he could demand anything of them. He developed a passion for the artillery: one always found him around the cannons, cleaning them, repairing them. He suggested improvements in their aiming, for their transportation. He wasn't far from loving them as real human beings. In reality, cannons were his only friends, just as they were of the Sergeant of Aurigni. Jean felt lonely, and yet he was not completely alone. Without his knowledge, his performance and his successes were carefully noted and included in voluminous reports regularly sent to Omer Bey, the inspector of the army who passed them on to the one who ordered them. From a distance, and without him suspecting anything, Jean's progress was being followed with the greatest attention.

Six years passed. Jean had become a war machine, disciplined, unwearying, efficient. But what had become of his soul? Perhaps he didn't know himself. One fine day, he found himself placed in the most prestigious regiment, charged with defending Cairo against a potential enemy attack. He did not understand how he had earned this sudden promotion, and neither did his superiors, in spite of the stripes that he was known to have won. His new barrack, situated in the heart of the citadel, was more airy, spacious and comfortable than the previous one. He also benefited from extensive privileges: he could enter and leave the citadel when he wished, go to the city and stay there all his free time. In short, he had much less to do. No enemy was going to approach to attack the capital, and work developed into a routine. With routine came boredom, and with boredom came the blues.

One evening after dinner, Jean found himself along with his comrades in the mess room. As was his habit, he kept to himself, lost in his daydreams, instead of taking part in their conversations. A pageboy, wearing the livery of the viceroy, entered the room and came up to him. He asked him to follow him. Surprised by this invitation and by the late hour, Jean followed the adolescent through the many rooms of the barracks until they reached a narrow staircase well concealed in the fortified wall. The pageboy instructed him to climb this and then disappeared. Jean complied. The stairs were steep, narrow and many. Somewhat breathless, he arrived at a vast room with such low ceilings that he could have touched it with his raised hands. Waiting for him there was a still-young man, to whom Omer Bey behaved in the most obsequious manner. Powerful but heavily built, he had blonde hair and blue eyes, a broad hooked nose, and constantly screwed up his eyes indicating bad eyesight. Jean recognized him immediately, for he saw him everyday at the parade that took place in the courtyard of the palace.

He was Dawood Pasha, the Viceroy of Egypt. He greeted Jean, 'You seem so lost in your so-very-melancholic thoughts that I said to myself that perhaps you needed some company, which is why have I sent for you.' Jean could not help himself from asking the Viceroy how he had read his thoughts. 'Quite simply because I was watching you. Follow me.' Dawood Pasha took Jean through a maze of galleries, corridors, passages, all narrow and with low ceilings, which ran over the barrack rooms and which, because of their narrow openings, were barely visible from below, allowing surveillance into the furthest corners of the building. This mezzanine served to spy on the military.

'Each barrack,' explained Dawood Pasha, 'is provided with the same architectural facilities. I use it often; it allows me to sniff out the state of mind of my soldiers. I have been watching you every evening for sometime now, and I have noticed your mood becoming grim. But come to my house, we will be more comfortable there.' Abandoning Omer Bey there, bent double, the most powerful man of Egypt took the increasingly surprised Jean along as if he were an old friend.

Leaving the barrack, they reached the enormous palace of the ruler of Egypt. They passed through the official part, almost deserted at this late hour. They got to the Selamlik, the part reserved for men, where lay the private apartments of the viceroys. He took Jean to a mezzanine decorated with slender columns, and a balcony from where one saw an enchanting view of the sleeping city and its surroundings bathed in a blue luminance. The Pasha clapped his hands and many pageboys appeared carrying a small carafe filled with raki, a strong liquor of the Middle East, as well as many glasses. They served beautifully worked tsimbuks to the Viceroy and Jean and the two men sat down on the low divans. Then Dawood Pasha began, 'It is obvious that I do not treat all officers in this manner, in fact the truth is that I never even get them here. You were brought to my attention by the reports that were submitted to me about you, just as they are about all the other officers in my army. Your qualities were so apparent that I had you transferred to the most envied regiment of the country, responsible for watching over my security. During the daily parades, you stood out from the others, by your height of course, but also by your appearance. I discussed this with Omer Bey and we both agreed. You most certainly come from an illustrious family. You are different from the others. I sensed it the instant I caught sight of you for the first time.

Then, to put Jean at ease, he recounted his past, 'I was born on the Dalmatian coast of Serbian and Christian parents. When I was very young, I was taken away from my parents by the recruiters of the army of our Padshah. I was forced to convert to Islam and sent to the corps of the Janissaries. Just like you did it for yourself, I also earned my stripes. What is good about the Ottoman Empire is that each one gets his chance without any prejudices based on class or nationality. I was twenty-seven-years old when Sultan Salim sent us to conquer Egypt, which was governed by the military classes of the Mamelukes. They put up a ferocious fight. We vanquished them, and our sultan was made the monarch of independent Egypt at the gates of Cairo. That was thirty years ago. I continued to climb the echelons. From the army, they transferred me into administration and sent me to govern the remote provinces. Then, one fine day, I returned to Egypt, this time as a representative of Allah's shadow on earth. It's a difficult job but a good one, to be the viceroy of Egypt. Now, tell me something about yourself.'

And so, Jean recounted his childhood near Mantoue. He described the murder attempt on him, an episode which enthralled Dawood Pasha. He continued with his capture by the pirates, which on the other hand, left his interlocutor completely indifferent. 'Tell me once again about the assassination attempt on you. You don't have any suspicions about the person or people behind this operation?'

Jean could only deny.

'I am certain that this bloody episode that took place is linked with the mystery of your origin. I cannot understand how you possess no indication, no clue that could possibly put you on the trail of your ancestors.'

'Yet, noble Pasha, it is the truth.'

The Viceroy became pensive. 'My job has trained me to assess men. I repeat, I am certain that you belong to a family of the highest rank and that your origin is illustrious. So then why this mystery?'

Jean was careful not to share Father Soragno's theory according to which he could be the legitimate son of the Commander of Bourbon. This secret, he decided he would not share with anyone at the moment.

'Are you happy?' Dawood Pasha asked him missing a beat.

'To tell you the truth, I miss the action.'

'Is there anything else?'

Jean's voice was barely audible, 'I am not free, noble Pasha.'

'A soldier's job seems to suit you, it puts no restriction on your movement, you can come and go to the city as you please.'

'Certainly, but I have not chosen the master I want to serve. He was imposed on me.' Dawood Pasha did not insist further, and with a few polite words, dismissed Jean.

Jean was charmed by the generosity of the Viceroy, and moved by his confidence. It was the first time that he felt like a complete man and not just a number in the army, it was the first time in six years that he made an intelligent and friendly contact with another human being who treated him as an equal.

The Pasha invited Jean again to his palace and this time he introduced him to his library. Huge, intricately-woven carpets covered the floor, low divans with rich brocade work were lined along the walls, weapons were hung on the walls, each more magnificent than the other. This display of weapons alternated with shelves that were piled with precious volumes. Jean was surprised to see that this old janissary had a passion for reading. The Viceroy read his thoughts and smiled, 'A soldier is not necessarily uncultured.' Attracted by the extensive knowledge of this bewildering man, Jean accepted his invitations, which were now almost everyday, with pleasure. Through the books from his collection, Dawood Pasha made Jean discover the treasures of Muslim culture, particularly history, medicine, and poetry. He also spoke to him about his future, suggesting without spelling it out that if he continued thus, he could rise to the highest of posts. 'But for that, you must embrace Islam.' To this idea, Jean rebelled. Dawood Pasha insisted: 'It is nothing more than a formality. No one is going to force you to go to the mosque. Even I do not go there unless it is unavoidable.' He explained to Jean that Islam did not limit itself to demanding rites, 'There is a lot more to our religion than that, in the sense that Islam can be the vehicle of a thinking very profound, more universal and more personal at the same time.'

Gradually, Dawood Pasha introduced Jean to Sufism, a vertiginous abstraction that mixed mysticism and poetry, metaphysical philosophy and faith, taking men to heights hitherto inaccessible, which had created exceptional thinkers who passed on this luminous culture from generation to generation. Under the tutelage of Dawood Pasha, Jean experienced an opening of horizons, the extent and the depth of which he had never imagined, and which attracted him like a magnet. At the same time, his ties with the Viceroy quite naturally became stronger. Sometimes he felt the latter's gaze dwell upon him with a strange expression.

One evening, Jean dared to ask the Viceroy a question which had been on his mind, 'Why do you favour me so much?'

'Very simply because I intend on making you my successor.'

'How do you know I will be worthy of that?'

'Because you possess all the necessary qualities. But there is only one obstacle, your refusal to convert to Islam. Come on, let yourself be circumcised, you will feel nothing. Once circumcised, it will be like you were already a Pasha.'

Jean smiled. 'We'll see,' he answered without compromising himself. In the meantime, he enjoyed the paternal affection of Dawood Pasha, an affection that, along with the teachings that he received, had suddenly given meaning to his life. A sentiment that went hand in hand with a growing temptation for the Orient.

Jean took full advantage each time of his visits into Cairo. At that time, the marvelous monuments left by the Mamelukes, the former rulers of Egypt, shone with all their radiance while next to them the best architects of the Ottoman Empire had built mosques and palaces in their own style. While walking in the caravanserai, in the madarsas, listening to the fountains which tinkled in every corner of the street in the sebils,[2] Jean surrendered increasingly to the charm of the place, a charm that was heightened even more by his visits to some houses tagged with a bad reputation. In discovering pleasure, his body had passionately responded to sensual feelings. He saw himself becoming Firangi Bey: Firangi, 'Frenchman' was the nickname given to him by his soldiers – and why not Firangi Pasha, living in a splendid palace, with the most well-provided harem, waging war here and there with fervour, and at night engaging in the intoxication of metaphysical speculation with the great Sufi masters. What beautiful revenge on his roots! A child without a name, a child isolated, ignored, abandoned to his solitude becoming the most prodigious ruler of Egypt.

More than anything, Jean loved the big bazaar of Cairo. This labyrinth was laid out over a number of places demarcated by guilds. Fruits and vegetable made his mouth water, flowers symbolic of Ottoman culture dazzled his view. Perfume sellers made him smell the rarest of smells. Tailors unrolled the most precious of fabrics while proposing custom-tailored kaftans and abayas to him. Jewellers flashed earring and bracelets, imploring him to adorn his wives with these. The crowd of buyers distracted him just as much. The Bedouins, in colourful gowns, who had never seen a European, would go wide-eyed looking at him. Jews, recognized by the yellow colour that they were forced to wear, stayed out of his way. Rich merchants with huge bellies passed majestically, flippantly shaking their flywhisks. Officers wearing turbans topped with very long feathers stopped at the bars. The wives of the rich and noble, completely veiled apart from their eyes, surrounded by their eunuchs, avidly inspected shop fronts. There were also Greeks, Italians, Circassians, and the Persians, recognizable by their national dress, and also black slaves sent to run errands. Jean noticed a woman leaving a jeweller's stall, covered in a cape up till her feet. Pale blue muslin was wrapped around her head but her face was uncovered, a sign that she was not a Muslim. Jean gathered that she was a Christian, a Copt.[3] He admired her fine features, her straight nose, but above all her big dark eyes, with a melancholic expression, protected by long eyelashes and arched eyebrows which were perhaps a shade too thick. An old woman of rare ugliness, probably her governess, and many servants followed her. Jean shivered as he watched her; he had never seen such a beautiful woman before. Sensing that she was being watched, she fixed her eyes on him. She didn't even give a shadow of a smile, but her eyes lit up for a second, then she turned and moved away. Jean did not dare follow her.

All night he dreamt of her, wondering how he could see her again. He couldn't find any other way apart from returning the next day to the jeweller's where he had seen her. An absurd measure, for it was highly unlikely that she would return to the same shop. Luck, however, was on his side: there she was again at the jeweller's stall. Jean stared at her for a long time through the window. For a moment, her eyes met his. She didn't seem to recognize him. Her purchases done, she came out and without even a look at Jean, she turned into the street, followed by her governess and her servants. Jean fell in behind them. Only once, the governess turned around, noticed him but said nothing. They then reached the end of the bazaar where a litter awaited the woman. Jean went towards her and stood there like a dunce looking at her get onto the litter. Once again, she didn't seem to notice him. The governess shot a piercing look at him but said nothing. The servants, at a gesture, lifted the litter and set out on their route. Quite naturally, Jean followed them. They walked for a long time as the Copts lived in the outlying areas of Cairo. They reached a very high and a very long wall concealing an important residence. The gate opened to let the litter pass but did not close after. Without hesitating, Jean entered. A fountain whispered in a courtyard covered with multi-coloured flowers and marbles. Descending from the litter, the woman climbed up the steps of an outside staircase. With a gesture, the governess asked Jean to follow her. Once upstairs, they passed through a long open gallery, at the end of which Jean, in the footsteps of the woman, entered a small room. The paneling was painted with fruits and flowers and the ceiling had golden stars, giving the room a festive air. As she was undoing her veils and her cape, the woman asked him:

'Captain Firangi, are you still a Christian?'

'How do you know my name?'

'A young foreigner, handsome and valiant, a favourite of the Viceroy, you see, the whole city knows of your existence. I repeat my question: Have you remained a Christian?' she said with a certain anxiety.

Jean reassured her on this point.

She asked, 'Why have you followed me?'

Jean didn't know how to respond, but his eyes were eloquent enough. She was probably in her forties and she was singularly attractive. She came close to him and softly kissed him on his lips. He took her in his arms, held her tight enough to choke her, and covered her with kisses. At first she let him continue, then suddenly she exploded. He had been mistaken by her melancholic air, she was a most ardent mistress.

And thus began the love affair of Jean and Latifa. When she was barely a woman, her parents had arranged for her marriage with a Copt who was much older than her and very rich, who practically never left his enormous estates in the Delta. Latifa paid him rare visits.

Every evening, after finishing his services, Jean ran to Latifa's house where the governess, the old and ugly Kahila, ushered him directly in. More and more frequently, he returned too late to his quarters to accept Dawood Pasha's invitations. The latter never posed any question nor ever made a remark. Nothing mattered more to Jean than Latifa. He had never imagined that a woman could be desirable to this extent ... and demanding. He left their stormy meetings fulfilled and shaky. Besides pleasure, his mistress also had a passion for confectioneries. Latifa never read, but she was intelligent and informed. Jean liked to converse with her in the rare interludes that she allowed him to. He appreciated her advice. To have acquired such knowledge of sensual pleasures, Jean supposed that she had a number of lovers. Was it to expiate 'the sins of the flesh' that she showed herself to be so religious? For apart from love and a weakness for sweet things, religion absorbed her. She often took Jean to the room that served as the chapel, where Copt priests chanted psalms while singing praises to the icons. Other pilgrims, passing through Cairo, stayed in Latifa's home. They came from Ethiopia. Their stories allowed Jean to hear about this Christian empire, mysterious and inaccessible by reputation, of which till now he had heard only vague stories.

Becoming bolder, Jean told Latifa about Dawood Pasha's promises of making him his successor, on the only condition that he became a Muslim. His mistress leapt up, her claws out: 'You want to renounce our Christianity! I will never see you again.'

'There was never any question. However, I have asked myself what my future would be, as a Christian officer.'

'Leave, leave the country!'

'You want to get rid of me for another lover?'

Latifa did not smile at the joke. Sadly, she replied: 'You deserve more than just being a slave.'

'I am no longer a slave, Latifa, I have achieved a high rank in the army, I have the Viceroy's trust. I can go and come wherever I wish...'

'Slave you were when you arrived here, slave you will remain, unless you spit on the cross and become a Muslim. Slave or a renegade, thus are your choices.'

Suddenly conscious of the reality, hidden by the mirage of the Orient, Jean felt devastated: 'How can I leave? I will become a defector who the entire police force of the country would be hounding after!'

'I will help you, for I prefer to lose you rather than see you lost. I have all it takes to buy the police, custom officers, ship captains of the country.'

Jean stepped out of his dark thoughts and looked surprised: 'You manage the fortune of your husband?'

'It is not about his money, but mine. I have inherited land not far from Cairo, in the valley of the Nile.'

Jean had explored the region on his horse. The valley, he had seen, was narrow and the property modest. 'The revenues from your land are actually enough?'

Latifa smiled: 'It is not the yield from my fields that makes me rich, it is the mummy.' She laughed at Jean's surprised expression: 'How come, after having lived for all these years in Egypt, you don't know what mummy is?' She explained that it was a thick brown liquid that oozed out of badly embalmed mummies of ancient Egypt. Upon contact with fresh air or with badly prepared aromates, they would stir up these secretions. For many years mummy had been the most fashionable elixir in Europe, and was thus very expensive. It came to be considered as a universal panacea and it was imported at a staggering price. 'The King of France,' added Latifa, 'has a huge consumption, he mixes it with rhubarb and gulps it to fight all the maladies he could possibly catch.... Now, my properties in the Nile valley are right next to an ancient necropolis. My peasants discovered hundreds of mummies and learnt to extract this source of fabulous richness. I close my eyes to their more or less legal trafficking and they give me the royalties, which make me financially independent from my husband.'

'You must be colossally rich if you are the only supplier of mummy in the country?'

'Alas, I am not the only one, we are many to ferociously compete with one another. Your friend, the Viceroy, has evidently never told you that he was the most rapacious man in Egypt. He keeps a close watch on our business and would be delighted to get his hands on it.'

Jean mused on all that was revealed to him by Latifa: 'So, it is the dead of ancient Egypt who will break the shackles of my slavery.'

Latifa pulled him towards her: 'Don't be in a rush. I need some time to organize your clandestine departure. In the meantime, live the last weeks of our happiness together to the fullest.'

However, the mummy and its extraction had turned on Jean's curiosity. He asked Latifa the favour of taking him there to see how the procedure actually took place. She seemed reluctant: 'Our peasants are very distrustful. They might not receive you very well.' Nevertheless, there was nothing she could refuse her lover, and sent for instructions to the superintendent of her property.

And thus, one fine morning, Jean left on an excursion accompanied by a few servants. Discretion held Latifa back from accompanying him. In Bulaq, they crossed the Nile on a felucca. They passed by the pyramids of Giza, across a cultured region shadowed by palm trees that swayed gently. They went past Sakara and its pyramid by degrees.

At the end of several hours, they reached a village with a miserable appearance bordering the desert at the extreme end of the cultivated zone. Despite Latifa's instructions, her superintendent received him without any warmth. As for the villagers, instead of welcoming him with the traditional hospitality of the Egyptian peasants, they turned away from him and went and shut themselves in their shacks. For many generations, they had preferred to despoil the graves rather than cultivate the land. They had dug out gold and precious objects that they sold for a bit of money, and above all, extracted mummy that they sold at ten times the price of gold. Any newcomer, including their mistress Latifa who rarely visited, was considered an intruder, and therefore a threat.

Meanwhile, the superintendent indicated the man responsible for collecting the mummy. He was like a beanpole, pale and so thin it was frightening, hirsute, unshaven, with a nose like an eagle's beak, long yellow teeth, with the eyes of a madman. Looking at his pupils, Jean immediately recognized the effects of kif, the hallucinogenic leaf of Egypt, which he had tried once or twice. Nevertheless, it was with a firm step that he took Jean and his servants into the desert. He noticed that the ground was strewn with debris that certainly came from graves, pieces of shrouds, masks, pottery, bones bleached by the centuries. The dunes, however, all looked the same and nothing indicated that they could be hiding anything of worth. Suddenly, a carved wall appeared, then a door covered in the sand, the beginning of a staircase sunk into the earth. Jean and the beanpole descended the stairs. The servants emphatically refused to follow them. They were sure that the tombs were full of djinns, of harmful genies. The beanpole lit a torch and went underground. Following him, Jean realized they were in an actual labyrinth of tunnels, sometimes narrow, sometimes very broad and very high, and many buried cathedrals. Lined there were stone sarcophagi with monolithic covers that were so heavy that the peasants had never succeeded in lifting them up. Piled up here and there were wooden sarcophagi, ripped open and shattered. There were hundreds, for, in fact, there was not one but many necropolises each adjoining one with the other. During a certain epoch, and for unknown reasons, the dead corpses had been put together in certain corners, which made for an almost endless reserve of mummy.

The beanpole made for the sarcophagi that he had decided to work on. He took the mummies out one by one and examined them quickly. Unless they were in good condition, he threw them aside with irritation. He knew that his treasure lay in those whose bandages were soaked with brownish stains in which he would make practiced incisions. A nauseating liquid began to ooze out which he delicately collected in glass jars. He asked Jean to give him a hand by getting the mummies he needed and putting away those that were of no use. Several hours passed, to the extent that Jean lost all sense of time. Was it morning, afternoon, or evening? He couldn't remember the time of the day they both had come underground. The air was unbreathable. The air was filled with different heavy smells. His head started to spin a bit. He found it more and more difficult to move. He felt an invisible weight on his shoulders forcing him to bend his knees and sit on the dusty floor. He surveyed the bas-reliefs of the tomb. Painted in bright colours, they depicted village scenes. The torch fixed on the wall illuminated their shadows, him and the beanpole who continued to leech his mummy. Completely absorbed in what he was doing, Jean saw the shadow-puppet of the raider of the tomb rise and come towards him. He raised a hand brandishing the dagger with which he extracted the mummy. Despite his drowsy state, Jean had the reflexes to roll over the floor to avoid the knife but the beanpole was already on him trying to stab him. Despite being less muscled, the drug had given him an unimaginable strength. With one hand, Jean tried to hold the knife that was unrelentingly going for his throat, and with the other he held the left hand of the beanpole. Briskly, with both his hands, he seized the armed wrist and with a desperate move, he turned it. The assassin was impaled upon his own weapon. He heaved a deep sigh, his eyes with the dilated pupils closed and he fell dead on Jean. Horrified and disgusted, Jean pushed the body away that, in spite of being thin, seemed surprisingly heavy to him. Too perturbed to ask himself any questions, he wiped the bloodstains from his clothes with some sand, found the exit and staggered up the steps. Outside, a starry night had fallen, and Latifa's servants awaited him patiently. They took their horses and rode at great speed to Cairo.

He went to his mistress who was waiting for him with her governess, and recounted everything to her. In retrospect, she panicked for Jean, but didn't seem particularly surprised. The daily contact with the dead had made her peasants completely bizarre, and the kif that the beanpole smoked had made it worse. Kahila, however, saw a dreadful omen in the incident. She bustled around, lighting incense and beeswax candles around Jean and gave him an amulet in the form of an eye, a distant after-effect of ancient Egyptian practices against fate. Though comforted by his mistress, Jean remained intrigued about the incident. The truth was that Latifa's explanations did not leave him entirely satisfied.

But soon other worries made him put out of his mind the assassination attempt on him. One day, he was forced to accept the evidence: a disturbing atmosphere reigned in the regiment. For some time now, he had suspected it but refused to admit, his conviction based more on fleeting impressions than on real suspicions. Finally, he had to admit that something was not right with the men: they appeared to be lazy, they grumbled for nothing, they remained indifferent to chastisements, be it the whip or the prison dungeon, that their negligence had called for. However, Jean noticed that the bad tempered heads could uniquely be counted amongst the Arabs of the regiment. Since the conquest of Egypt by the Ottomans thirty years ago, hostility had grown between the Turks, the occupant, and the Arabs of Egypt, the occupied. The former blamed the latter for being lazy and less reliable, the latter accused the former of being bad Muslims – for the Ottomans showed tolerance towards other religions. The occupants, to protect themselves, had limited the number of Arabs admitted in the elite regiments like the one in which Jean served. And yet, without realizing, for many years now, Arabs had infiltrated these regiments, without any real purpose but simply because they had higher salaries.

In the following weeks, the situation only got worse. The Arabs Jean commanded became really intolerable, although to him they personally expressed a sincere sympathy and a deep devotion. They became more and more insolent with the other officers, the Turks, and Jean was surprised to see the latter not notice it. Many a times, he thought of talking about it with Dawood Pasha and anticipated doing it at the first occasion.

One morning, the programme entailed a march in the desert, which was separated from the citadel only by a deep artificial pit. Jean, at the head of his men, crossed the bridge and took to the trail, which went straight towards the south. For a few days now, the khamsin had been posing a threat, those sand winds that paralyzed the entire country, but above all, made everyone nervous and irritable. Jean, marching next to his men, found himself level with a certain Tariq.

He was a big, handsome, robust fellow, with large brown eyes, who had something of a mad man about him. He also came across as a true master and a born commander. He probably came from a big local family that had fallen to extreme poverty. 'Listen to me, maalem,'[4] he whispered. 'We are hungry, we are paid miserably whereas the Turks get much better pay than us and have all the advantages. This cannot continue.' Jean could not find words to reply because he knew Tariq was right: the Arab soldiers were underpaid. Encouraged by this silence, Tariq continued, 'We have decided to ask Dawood Pasha for a raise, and if he does not agree, we'll kill him.' Jean hid his distress while keeping his silence. 'Join us. You are different from the others, and on top of that, you are a Christian. Join us and you will benefit from it. We will find fortune and you, you will win your freedom,' said Tariq.

Finally, Jean managed to say, 'How do you plan to attack the Viceroy? He is always surrounded by his guards and his staff.'

Tariq sniggered, 'Except during the morning examination.' This one took place early every morning in the area that lay in front of the palace. Not feeling the need for any special protection in the best-protected compound of Egypt, Dawood left his home, almost alone, climbed a podium and inspected the men. Jean regained his poise and said, 'Do not commit this foolishness, I will talk to the Viceroy, and you will receive this raise without any difficulty.'

'He will refuse to listen to you.'

Jean didn't insist further, for he agreed whole-heartedly with the rebel: Dawood Pasha listened to no one. 'Most of all do not execute your plan. You have no chance of winning and you all will be massacred.'

Tariq responded through his teeth: 'We will act in three days. You alone can open all doors for us, but in any case, we are going to act with or without you. If you betray us, you will be killed… But no, I know you won't give us away, I know you too well, maalem.' Tariq said no more. Once again, he looked straight at the line of the horizon of the desert towards which the men marched with rapid steps.

Jean found himself facing a cruel dilemma. He knew that the Arab soldiers were right, and he felt a deep sympathy for them. He loved his men and he knew that he was loved by them, and he didn't want to betray them. On the other hand, he could not just leave his protector, his mentor, who had shown him much generosity and solicitude, be mistreated and probably assassinated in front of his eyes. To put him on his guard, to warn him, would be to send Tariq and his accomplices to their deaths.

On the eve of the fateful day, he was invited by the Viceroy to spend the evening at his library. He was constantly distracted, preoccupied, barely listening to his host compare Arabic poetry with Persian poetry at length. About twenty times he almost gave away the plot that threatened him, and twenty times he failed to make up his mind. Finally, and though very late, he addressed the issue troubling his mind. He explained that the money they received was clearly insufficient and that it should be raised if one wanted to avoid serious problems. With an indolent gesture of his ivory handled flywhisk, Dawood Pasha chased away this matter of concern as if he were chasing away an insect: 'I think you are mistaken, but for your sake, I shall think about it in desired time,' and before Jean could insist, he sent him off with his natural courtesy.

At night, Jean found it impossible to sleep, but he did come up with an idea. At dawn, he returned to the palace. Dawood Pasha always woke up very early. As if he were awaiting him, Jean found him in his office, surrounded by his scribes writing down orders and receiving his colleagues. Jean knew that if the Viceroy was held up with some administrative work as early as seven in the morning, it would be one of the lieutenants who would attend the parade. He had thus prepared a series of questions concerning his regiment to discuss with Dawood Pasha. There was nothing unusual about it, except that this morning, he added an almost infuriating slowness to it. He discussed, quibbled, made propositions, drew up obstacles. Dawood Pasha responded with a commendable patience, didn't seem to be in a hurry and took all his time. Jean was beginning to believe he had won the case when, suddenly, Dawood Pasha got up: 'It is almost 7 o'clock, I am going down to attend the parade,' and he shot a smile at Jean which he would have liked to believe charming but in which he detected a scathing irony. Jean leapt behind him. He had decided to protect him, even if it meant his own death. Once in the courtyard, Dawood Pasha climbed on top of the podium, and Jean stood in front of him. The march began. From the corner of his eye, he easily spotted Tariq, who approached at the head of his detachment. Arriving in front of the podium, Tariq let out a yell. Hundreds of Arab soldiers rushed towards the Viceroy with him. Swords raised, they surrounded the podium. Tariq, in a commanding tone and a powerful voice, spoke: 'Pasha! Hear our request. We want a raise in our pay.'

Dawood only had to be crafty, procrastinate, and make a promise to calm them and then later punish them. Instead, he roared: 'Back off, you despicable creatures, take your places, sons of bitches!' and he launched into a string of insults each more offensive than the other. Enraged, the soldiers sprang on him. Jean didn't have the time to draw his sword. He saw the assailants collapse, pierced by multiple arrows. In a minute, the terraces overlooking the compound were covered with archers who were aiming at the rebels. Tariq was the first to fall.

Immediately after, the site was invaded by the Ottoman guards who at the orders of Dawood Pasha, arrested the Arab soldiers. Innocent or guilty, all, until the last one, were unrestrainedly decapitated. While Jean trembled with emotion and horror, the Viceroy remained impassive in the face of this slaughter. Finally, he fired a last order that the heads of the rebels were to be exhibited on the walls of the citadel to set an example. He then withdrew with dignity, lifting the tail of his embroidered abaya, to save it from getting dirty by the blood that had soaked the sand of the courtyard. He signalled Jean to follow him. While passing through the rooms of the palace, he addressed him in a soft voice, 'I understand that you must be surprised, but you must know that I was aware of everything from the beginning. Isn't it my job to be well informed? I am lucky to have excellent spies everywhere. To tell you the truth, I myself have trained and placed them.'

Jean lost his temper, 'Instead of massacring those good soldiers, why didn't you prevent their revolt, simply by granting them a raise, as soon as you learnt of their dissatisfaction?'

'Precisely because it was already too late by the time I learnt of it. I could have perhaps calmed them down this time, but they would have revolted later, for another reason. The virus of rebellion had grown in them and it was impossible to put it out. I did not hesitate to put my own life in danger to let the revolt break so that the repression that I ordered served as a salutary example that would calm all temptations of this kind for a long time.' He let Jean digest his response, then he picked up where he had left: 'I also wanted to know how you would react. I was not ignorant of the fact that the rebels had asked you to join them.' He stopped and fixed Jean with an unfathomable look that somehow made him shudder. 'Around me, no one would have appreciated your silence regarding this, they would have seen it as a lack of devotion, if not treachery.' And abandoning Jean there, he picked up his walk with calculated steps.

His insidious tone, his words charged with menace, alarmed Jean. Neglecting the work that awaited him in the barrack, he left the palace with quick steps and got out of the citadel. He covered in record speed the quite long distance that separated him from Latifa's home. Like always he knocked on the small door on the side. No one answered. He noticed that the door was ajar. As he entered he felt the thickest of silence reigned there. He crossed the garden to the rooms on the ground floor. Not only were they deserted but they had been completely disfurnished. He went up a floor and found the same situation. During the night, the house had been emptied and abandoned. Distraught, Jean could not believe what he was seeing. He even went down to the cellars where he heard a faint noise. Because of the light coming in from the cellar window, he discovered Kahila, the governess, huddled up in a corner. 'Don't be afraid, Kahila, it is me,' Jean whispered. She got up with pain, she could barely walk and her face was covered in bruises. She had been brutally beaten. Jean managed to help her climb up. He brought her to the garden, found a jar of water and softly washed her face. She hastened to tell him but had difficulty talking: 'He came last night, the black eunuch, asking to see the master who had arrived earlier, unannounced, called by a mysterious letter. Master and the eunuch shut themselves into a room. Then the eunuch left as fast as he had arrived. The master, in an indescribable state of anger, taking four steps at a time, entered my mistress's room and beat her even more violently than me. He then dragged her, more dead than alive, to the road and forced her inside the palanquin. They went back to his felucca that awaited them in Bulaq and left for his estates in the Delta. He ordered the servants to completely empty out the house and to carry everything to the country for he had decided to never return to the city.'

'But why? What has he done with your mistress?' Jean asked distraught.

The old governess said with a sly expression: 'I don't know, but during that horrific incident when he was beating her up, he repeatedly said that she was nothing but a whore and that he was going to make her regret all her life that she cheated on him with a filthy foreigner.'

It was clear to him that they had been denounced. 'That black eunuch, who came last evening to talk to your master, you know him?'

'I have often seen him in the bazaar, he's the big eunuch from the Viceroy's harem.'

Jean couldn't believe it. So the Viceroy had a constant watch on him and had learnt of his affair with Latifa. But why this denunciation? In no time the truth become clear to him: as long as Jean had frequented the illicit houses of Cairo, Dawood Pasha had no complaints, but he didn't approve of Jean falling in love with a woman. Perhaps he was behind the bizarre assassination attempt on him by the beanpole collector of the mummy. Jean felt forced to admit to himself that the Viceroy was quite simply jealous of him.

He stepped out of his thoughts to ask Kahila: 'Tell me where are your master's estates. I am going to free Latifa and bring her back with me.'

'Don't count on it, Captain Firangi, you won't be able to get close to it. Master has ordered that she be guarded day and night. Any stranger found prowling around will be killed without warning. Before being forcibly taken away, my mistress had the time to slip in a message for me: I had to wait for you here and tell you that she will always love you but that, if you wanted her to live, you must on no account attempt to free her or even to see her again. She added that Dawood Pasha was as angry as a cheated woman with him, that he was looking to get his revenge and that you had no other choice but to leave Egypt as soon as possible.' Then Kahila began to complain. The master, after having beaten her, fired her. 'He told me he'll kill me if he ever saw me again. I don't know where to go. I have nothing.' This was something Jean highly doubted. So many years in the service of someone as generous as Latifa would have generated fat savings. Nevertheless, Jean gave to her the full purse that was always on him. She quickly seized it, hid it in her layers of cloth, and continued to complain without thanking him.

As fast as he could, Jean left the house that had become so ghostly. He returned to the citadel taking slow steps so as to give him time to think and decide. He went straight to the barrack, and after giving an unimportant excuse for being late, joined in his service, as if nothing had happened.

Jean had to wait for nightfall and for the lights of the barrack to be extinguished to act. His plan required speed and precision. His perfectly timed schedule rested on the certainty of not being invited this evening by Dawood Pasha. However, he was. A pageboy came to tell him that the Viceroy was waiting for him in the Selamlik of the palace. Jean went there full of apprehension, wondering what this man had in store for him, this man who was the most powerful in Egypt, upon whom Jean had incurred disapproval, jealousy, and hatred.

Dawood Pasha welcomed him more kindly than usual. During the course of the evening, he made no allusions, neither to the revolt of the Arab soldiers, nor to Latifa. He gleefully embarked upon the meanderings of knowledge. He recounted the minor details of the life of his hero, the Sufi poet Jalaluddin Mevlana, who had lived in the heart of Turkey, in Konya, a hundred years ago. He went over his strange friendship with Chams, another Sufi master, in his sixties and bilious. He recited some poems of Rumi. Whenever his memory failed him for a minute, he went looking for the volume in the shelves of the library. Dawood Pasha was as good a narrator as those at crossroads who unwound the epics in front of their dumbstruck audience. Meanwhile, Jean, consumed by anxiety, was incapable of being attentive. He had to make a tremendous effort to look captivated. To the charm expended by his mentor, he tried to respond with a lightness that entailed a lot of feigning. In addition, the Sufi wisdom coupled with the outrageous cruelty displayed the same morning, left him cold. Inside, Jean was boiling with impatience, and yet, as if on purpose, Dawood Pasha held him later than usual. He sent him back graciously, making him promise to be back the next evening. Jean thanked him profusely, bowed respectfully and took his leave. He conspicuously crossed the rooms of the Selamlik, barely lit, but reaching the door, he didn't leave. He turned around, careful not to make any noise, and hiding himself in the darkness, retraced his steps. He quietly passed by the slightly open door of Dawood Pasha's library. He saw him put aside his tsimbuk, his long pipe filled with amber at the end, to bury himself in a thick work that he had pulled out from the shelf. He raised his head as if he heard something and Jean froze. But no, an idea had come to him for he plunged back into his obscure writings.

Stealthily, he went towards the Viceroy's office, the topography of which he knew perfectly. He reached the room where his secretaries worked which, of course, at this hour was deserted. He lit an oil lamp, took one of the paper sheets from a desk and quickly scrawled a travel order on it. The document in hand, he went over to the neighbouring desk, which was the one where Dawood Pasha worked, and found on a low table, next to his favourite sofa, a stamp in agate and gold that served as his signature. He stamped it on the mission order. He left the office and walked out of the palace. The sentries, who had known him for a long time, let him pass.

Jean went towards the barrack with the intention of gathering his belongings. The precautions that he had taken would save him from being located. But, on the other hand, he saw soldiers of the Viceroy's personal security cordon off the exits of the barrack. Others were entering noisily, breaking open doors, knocking over furniture, screaming at officers and soldiers, rummaging everywhere. He heard them yell asking where Captain Firangi was hiding. He understood that, during the evening, Dawood Pasha had showed the extent of his hypocrisy to better strike immediately after and have him arrested. The time that he took to forge the travel order had saved him, for otherwise the Viceroy's guards would have found him in the barrack and thrown him in the slammer to await worse to arrive. So while the guards continued to look for him in the barrack, Jean headed as fast as possible towards the gate of the citadel. At this hour of the night, it was closed. He produced his fake travel order to the officer on duty. The latter knew the seal of the Viceroy. He opened the small emergency door called the hole in the needle, pierced in the big gate. Jean bent to pass through it and found himself outside the citadel in the luminous night.

Heading towards the south of Cairo, he passed a region that was half abandoned where ruins of monuments, open-air turbés[5] stood. Jean passed by the considerable remains of the mosque edified by Amr, the conqueror who brought Islam to Egypt. He reached Fostat, a modest quarter isolated from the city, where Greek, Armenian and Syrian monasteries were grouped and where his walks had many times taken him.

On the banks of the Nile, a few feluccas were lined up. Jean went to each one of them but the sailors had gone home and everyone around was asleep. Jean had no way of escaping from Cairo. He would inevitably be found and arrested. He had seen enough of Dawood Pasha in action to realize that the latter was not going to burden himself with misgivings before striking. He expected at all times to hear the gallop of riders in his pursuit. While waiting, the deepest of silence surrounded him.

A noise from a felucca pulled him out of his thoughts. He hadn't inspected it well, for the last boat had a sleepy captain who went right back to sleep. Jean pounced on the sailor and woke him rather rudely. The latter grumbled obscenities but opened his eyes; he recognized the uniform that Jean was wearing, which made a big impression. He once again produced his travel order, which the sailor was completely incapable of reading, but knowing how to recognize an official document, he submitted to Jean's orders. Soon he raised the sail, and with the first light of dawn that appeared on the horizon, the felucca moved south.

Jean was very careful while reaching the port of Bulaq, for barely had his disappearance been discovered by the Viceroy's guards and the alert sent out, that the hunt turned principally towards the north, in other words on the routes of Alexandria and the path of the Nile. All feluccas of the Bulaq port were carefully searched.

But why south? The north was being very closely watched. West had the infinitely extending desert populated with ferocious tribes. Muslims occupied the east. Only the south remained, where, far away, commenced the Christian empire of Ethiopia whose priests had spoken to Jean. For decades now, this empire had been on a latent war situation with Egypt. Dawood Pasha had just sent an army from Cairo meant to go fight the Ethiopians. The fake travel order that Jean had forged for himself commanded him to join this expeditionary body. He was convinced that once there, he would find a way to prove his identity to the brothers of his religion.

During the course of the years when he had been immersed in his military career in the Egyptian Army, Jean had never fully accepted his fate. Often he had thought of escaping. For a long time, this eventuality remained out of question because he was watched rather too closely. But ever since the doors had been opened, this need had become more accessible. A well-respected officer, the Viceroy's favourite, with promises of higher duties, he still remained a slave, just as Latifa had said. He could do nothing for the woman he still loved, apart from following her command to run away. He could only hope that fate would be mild towards the mistress he had been forced to abandon. He also knew that the pretty Copt could count on her own resources and her strong mind. The deceit that he suffered at the hands of Dawood Pasha, revealing the latter's true face of cynicism, jealousy and cruelty, had wiped away all his last hesitations.

Another element played an important role in his state of mind during this dramatic day. He realized that since his birth, circumstances had completely and exclusively driven his life. Not only had he never known true freedom but also he never had the right to free will. He thus decided to take his destiny in his own hands. From the moment the sun appeared behind a cliff and spilled into the waters of the Nile with an orange tint, he felt a profound sense of elation. He had succeeded in escaping and he had left behind his past full of constraints. Nothing held him back, he was free, free, free.

Going up the Nile, the felucca passed Minya, Asyout, Luxor, Aswan. Arriving at the first waterfall on the Nile, they abandoned the felucca, and like many other travellers, went ahead on foot against the river's current. Higher up, they found another felucca that took them towards the south. It sailed through a mineral desert where the white sand mixed with black volcanic rocks. In this desolation rose pyramids built by African pharaohs. At Atbara, Jean abandoned the Nile for one of its tributaries, heading towards the northwest of Ethiopia, his destination. As they proceeded, navigation became more and more difficult, rocks started showing on the surface, and sandbanks multiplied.

One beautiful morning, the Sudanese who was conducting the felucca refused to go any further. The region was unsanitary, tribes revolted and had sown the seeds of death here. Jean tried to offer him all the money he had but the Sudanese was afraid. Jean decided to continue on foot, alone. The Sudanese begged Jean not to do this. He proposed that he return to take on the course of Nile again till Khartoum, then go back up one of its branches to the west of Ethiopia. Jean refused, he did not want to take a step back. Going back would mean returning to slavery.

Thus, he left, guiding himself vaguely, thanks to a compass. Very soon, he realized the Sudanese was right: he was moving ahead in a region that seemed endless, rather flat, sandy, where nothing but thorny shrubs devoid of leaves grew. Sometimes, he had to go to the bottom of a dried river stream to painfully climb a slope, cutting his hands and feet on jagged rocks. Nothing could have been more monotonous, more depressing than this land, but above all, it produced neither water nor food. Jean met not a single rebellious nomad, and very soon was struck by hunger and even more by thirst. From time to time, he found an old water source where a little bit of muddy and foul smelling water had dried up at the bottom of the clay. He pulled out roots of some of the plants that grew all around and chewed them with disgust. Fatigue added to his misfortunes. Each step became more difficult, and even though he didn't want to stop he had the impression that this would lead to death. He strengthened his will power and put one foot ahead of the other, more and more slowly, more and more heavily. His legs were giving away, his whole body trembled, but he continued to walk. He knew that straight ahead, far away, freedom awaited him. His body refused to obey him. Despite himself, his body collapsed. Was he going to fail so close to his goal? Was he freed of the weight that oppressed him since his birth to die stupidly of hunger and thirst in a desert? He had to find the strength to continue at all costs. He managed to lift himself once, twice, and move forward a few steps. On the third fall, he remained stretched out, immobile, his fevered mind falling asleep to memories, images and visions. Even though he had kept his eyes open and morning had only just begun, suddenly, everything around him seemed to be drowning in the thickest of darkness. Then he knew he had to succumb. At least, he told himself, he wouldn't die a slave but a free man. He managed to murmur, 'Blessed Virgin, have pity on me,' and sunk into unconsciousness.

1 The Ottoman sultan.
2 Fountains meant to refreshen the passersby.
3 The Coptic Church is one of the oldest if not the most oldest branch of Christianity. It was born in Egypt. The Copts assert that the language they use in their liturgy is ancient pharaonic Egyptian of the hieroglyphs.
4 Chief.
5 Islamic funerary monument in the form of a dome-shaped mosque.

Ethiopia 1547

When Jean opened his eyes, he was almost blinded by a big rectangle of light, then he could make out some men and women bent over him. They were all very tall and very thin, with lots of frizzy hair. Almost naked, men carrying long spears and women draped in multicoloured fabric looked at him intensely. He was in a huge box and the rectangular light was its opening. He recoiled, then attempted to get up. Two women helped him up and made him swallow a potion. He fell asleep immediately after.

Little by little, he understood that he had been found comatose by the natives who had saved him and were looking after him well. He had actually been in the jaws of death and was slowly regaining his strength. During his recuperation, which took a while, he had ample time to observe life around him. These members of a semi-immobile tribe inhabited a region that was hard and ungenerous. They compensated for their poverty by showing deep generosity, an extraordinary skill to adapt to their demanding environment. They were prudent with their means and organized about the smallest of things. It requires a certain genius to live in this region and Jean was able to get a measure of it. Along with the gratitude towards those who had taken care of him he developed great respect for them. The local people appreciated that and showed genuine affection for him.

One day an Ethiopian monk appeared in their village dressed all in white. He was coming back from a pilgrimage to Jerusalem, the holy city to which Ethiopian Christianity had rights. He was returning to his convent in the heart of the Ethiopian Empire. Jean asked him, by gestures, to take him there. The monk accepted. Goodbyes with the members of the tribe were full of emotions on both sides. The natives offered all kinds of supplies for the journey, not hesitating to part with their belongings for their guest. Then the two men set off on the path of reddish sand.

During long and terrible weeks, they crossed the same kind of savannah where he had almost died of hunger and thirst. However, the monk was used to the terrain. He knew where to find a water source. Instead of consuming the supplies given by the natives, he preferred to feed on roots, but unlike Jean, he knew how to choose the more nourishing plants. Nevertheless, the gruesome heat, aridity of the soil, and unexpected difficulties that they encountered made their advance slow and painful.

Progressively, they saw the landscape rise into rounded hills. These were soon followed by higher and higher mountains. They were forced to go down deep valleys before climbing up steep slopes where the paths always became narrower and narrower. However, the temperature had fallen and greenery had begun to surface and Jean felt a huge relief. One day, they saw the horizon blocked by elongated mountains that seemed impassable. But the monk found the passes. It was freezing cold and Jean wondered how his companion in his pristine draperies managed the almost glacial temperature. Reaching the other side of the mountain, they entered into the heart of Ethiopia, a region of high plateaus where cultures overlapped by degrees and where rivers wound in the depths of large valleys. Jean noticed that the monk stopped often to observe their surroundings, and devised detours to find shelter under trees or under the shadows of rocks. His guide explained to him that the lords of the Muslim war had invaded this region and currently occupied the entire north of Ethiopia.

These precautions did not prevent them from falling into an ambush. They were moving forward, half bent between shrubs that reached their shoulders, when, springing out of nowhere, dozens of men attacked and neutralized them in no time. They were taken to a camp hidden in the pit of a small valley. The chief came to inspect them. The monk was ordered to be executed without any hesitation, but his companion intrigued him. It was not everyday that one saw a European in these regions, moreover one dressed in the tattered uniform of the Ottoman Army. So, not knowing what to do with him, he barked out an order. Four of his soldiers surrounded the two prisoners, and in a rather rude manner, enjoined them to head out on the road.

For several days, they were compelled to walk without knowing where they were going. In a hurry to conclude their mission, the guards gave them hardly any food, and allowed them little sleep. Exhausted, the two prisoners arrived in the camp of the Ottoman Army, the same that Jean according to his travel order was supposed to join. It was an important contingent responsible for forming the troops of the local princes, which were to attack the Christian empire of Ethiopia. Jean immediately took out the document that he had fabricated and was received with open arms. The Turkish officers, who detested the natives, assured him that there were never enough men to fight the Ethiopians and above all to discipline their local allies. The first thing that Jean did was to save the monk's life, who the Turkish wanted to behead. He explained to them that the monk had guided him to them, and so, without much difficulty, they released him. The monk didn't pray much for himself before disappearing.

Much as his official comrades warmly welcomed Captain Firangi, the favourite of the Viceroy, Jean immediately felt an instinctive dislike towards their commander. Short, ugly, swarthy, with small eyes gleaming with ruses and maliciousness, he compensated for an inferiority complex with arrogance. He addressed Jean with an abrupt tone: 'Why did you choose the path of the desert to join us, instead of following the track we ourselves followed, which means by land till Suez, then felucca till the port of Suakin, which has become our base only a little while ago, then once again on foot, but through the regions occupied by our friends? You should have fallen in behind to find us.' Jean was not about to tell him that he had certainly not taken this path, which, once his escape had been discovered, was immediately put under surveillance. Messengers galloped day and night distributing his description that could lead to his arrest. He replied in a loud voice,

'I wanted to take the shortest path. I was in a hurry to join my post.' However, such zeal didn't seem to convince the commander. Jean immediately saw suspicion rise in him. He pretended to believe him but from then on he was under an invisible surveillance night and day, and at the slightest provocation, he would be arrested, in which case he preferred not to imagine his fate. The commander sent a courier to Cairo, which no doubt was meant to inform Dawood Pasha of Jean's arrival and asking for instructions concerning him. Jean had time till the return of the courier, in a few weeks, to find a solution.

In between, treated as a choice recruit, he was put in charge of the artillery that composed of outdated cannons. Several officers were appointed to assist him… and also keep an eye on him. He could not show reluctance in the face of this huge task, working till late in the night to improve the artillery. The Muslim army moved forward toward the Tana Lake around which the Ethiopian Christian empire was laid out. The Turks tried to get along with the troops of the princes who moved ahead in the biggest disorder. They had entered the province of Wadj when the scouts came announcing that the Ethiopian Army was very close. The Turkish commander ordered the troops to stop and put up a camp. The next day, dawn had barely set in when Jean finished putting on his armour. His impossible situation was eating him up: he was responsible for spreading death amongst the Ethiopians when all he dreamt of was joining their camp. And yet, his determination whipped up his energy. Whatever happened, he had decided that before the day ended, he would reunite with his Christian brothers.

The Muslims expected to find the Ethiopians in the hills towards which they were heading, when suddenly, at the exit of the woods which sheltered their camp, they caught sight of the Ethiopian Army arranged in battle order on the other side of the valley. The spectacle was terrifying, but also magnificent, for the sun made the shields gleam from a distance and the thousands of Ethiopian pennants shimmer in the light. Despite the distance, Jean could make out the young Emperor Galadewos with a large battle-flag embroidered with a lion in gold, flapping next to him. His gaze running over the Ethiopians from far off, he was startled and couldn't hide expressing amazement to the

Turkish commander: 'I cannot be dreaming, I see European uniforms amongst the Ethiopians, officers, soldiers... who are they?'

'The Portuguese,' growled the commander, 'the Ethiopians, who are incapable of defending themselves all alone, called them for help, but the Portuguese took a long time to respond, to the point that we were all convinced that they would never come. But they have committed a serious mistake, because we will crush them like we will crush the Ethiopians.' The Portuguese, the Ethiopians, very close... Jean trembled with hope. But there was no time to lose.

Both the armies advanced towards one another. Once the Ethiopians were at a reasonable distance, Jean ordered his army to open fire. He had placed his artillery on a hill and skillfully aimed his cannons... to spare the Ethiopians. The first batch of cannonballs fell on the sides of the Christian troops. Jean swore, screamed at his artillerymen, and made them adjust their shots. The cannonballs got closer to the Ethiopians, but without reaching them. The Turkish officers who surrounded them grumbled. Jean realized that they didn't believe his errors, they suspected him of deliberately protecting the Christian soldiers and they were going to make him regret it. Jean had only a few minutes to do something. And yet he could not make himself open fire on his Christian brothers.

But suddenly, the battle that had started well for the Muslims took an ugly turn. The indisciplined troops of the local princes, too rushed, and fell into the swamps which lined the bottom of the valley. Thus trapped, the Ethiopians killed them at point blank range with long spears. Encouraged by this success, they went around the swamps and made a dash for the rest of the Muslim troops. The latter, demoralized, retreated, before taking flight. The Ethiopians went after them and massacred them. An entire regiment of Ethiopian cavalrymen galloped towards where Jean had installed his artillery.

He saw them coming towards him at full speed. The cavalryman who commanded the regiment raised his arm and threw his spear. Jean had only a fraction of a second to move away: it cut his shoulder instead of going through the middle of his chest. He fell on the ground. Immediately after, he felt hands violently tying him and dragging him away. The Ethiopians had taken him a prisoner. They systematically killed all Muslim soldiers, but spared the officers. Along with them, Jean, his shoulder bleeding heavily and causing grave pain, was dragged with rage and violence to the camp of Emperor Galadewos. Each tent of the armed forces were in different coloured canvases, some in red or blue, others in green and yellow, and had long flowing flames on top. Surrounding the tents of the 'chiefs' were those of the princes, recognizable by their large zebra-striped pavilions and enormous war-drums placed at their doors. A canvas wall, three metres high, formed the surrounding wall of the imperial quarter. Jean and the other prisoners were locked in an open air space, bound by a circle of thorny branches which had sharply pointed spears sticking out towards the tied prisoners.

On the floor like others and burnt under the sun, his wound still open and bleeding, Jean felt the last of his strength abandoning him. Despair held him by the throat: he had finally found his Christian brothers only to be treated like a diehard enemy by them. Instead of welcoming him with open arms, they promised him a dreadful fate, which Jean didn't doubt would be an outcome of his imprisonment. Thus, stronger than ever before, returned the conviction that he was born under an unfortunate star. In reality, life was not worth the trouble of staying alive; it was better to accept death that awaited him. A noise of drums and fifes pulled him out of his feverish torpor. He saw a troop of soldiers march, with swords drawn, running more than walking, followed by a band of musicians. Behind them, marching at the same speed, were guards carrying a canopy whose long red curtains completely concealed the chevalier riding underneath it. He could barely make out the white horse on which he was riding. Men on horses, carrying small pikes wrapped around in tufts of horse hair, dyed in red or in blue, concluded the procession that swarmed into the imperial quarter, and disappeared in a flash behind the canvas wall. Jean realized the conqueror of the day had just passed, Emperor Galadewos.

A little later, the branches that formed the door of their prison opened. Ethiopian soldiers came inside, seized the prisoners with the same brutality one by one to take them to the imperial quarter. The first to be taken was the Turkish commander, the vanquished of the day, then the officers, and then finally the chiefs of the local army. No one came back. Jean was saved for the last, intentionally. When the Ethiopian soldiers came for him, instead of allowing himself to be dragged like an animal to a slaughterhouse, he gathered the strength to stand on his feet and walk despite his shackles and his wounds. On entering into the compound of the imperial quarter, Jean recoiled: in front of him was strewn out a carpet of dead bodies. Emperor Galadewos showed no mercy. Already, at the end of the battle, he had all the soldiers killed, even those who had surrendered. Not a single Muslim combatant survived.

Pushed by the soldiers, avoiding stumbling upon the bodies, Jean went up to the throne. Emperor Galadewos sat on brocade cushions. He was barely twenty-five years old. The prominent chin hidden behind a thin beard, the hooked nose, the frowning eyebrows and the contemptuous grin made him look old. On his head, he wore a high crown in gold and silver, and held in his hands a big cross with fine gold work on it. A blue veil concealed the lower part of his face. A voluminous cloak of deep red velvet, fully embroidered in gold enveloped him.

Galadewos fixed his cold and hard look on the last surviving prisoner. He even got up to observe him from closer like a curious dog, and Jean noticed that he was quite short. His eyes gleamed while he scrutinized him for a long moment. Jean also saw, amongst the Ethiopian dignitaries clustered around the throne, some Portuguese officers, and above all, seated next to the Emperor on a lower throne, was a woman with a serious face. From her authoritative aura and her majestic posture, he guessed she was a princess of the imperial family.

Finally, the Emperor spoke in Asmari, his language, which a Portuguese officer translated in French. 'You are visibly a European. You certainly have renounced your religion to be sent to fight us.' Jean, stung by the insult, stood up straight and replied in a dry tone: 'I have never given up the true faith.'

'You are capable of cooking up a story to save your life. But a lie will be of no use to you, and will only add to your crimes. You are to be the object of the ultimate execution of this victorious day, but also of that which will bring me the most satisfaction.' Following a signal from him, the soldiers threw themselves on Jean to bring him towards the executioner waiting for him with a bloody sword in his hand.

Before being forced into it, Jean knelt down and held out his neck. At the same moment, an injunction thrown by a feminine voice froze the moment. Jean got up: the words that came out were from the princess seated next to the Emperor. She leaned towards the latter and had a long and vehement discussion with him. Galadewos listened to her with frowning eyebrows, with an apparent exasperation. Finally, he seemed to resign himself and barked out a violent order in return. The executioner sheathed his sword. The Portuguese officer explained to Jean that the Emperor had withheld his execution to examine his case again. He was put back in the enclosure that served as the prison and of which, from now on, he was the sole occupant.

At nightfall, torches were lit all around so that the prisoner, under constant surveillance, had no opportunity of escape. Soon after, he saw a procession approaching. He recognized the woman heading the procession; it was the princess who had saved his life by withholding his execution. A full mouth, her small eyes black and piercing, a massive nose and a large jaw, one could tell that she was used to command. A blue veil enwrapped her head, with her frizzy hair jutting out. She was followed by her women as well as by a Portuguese officer.

With a gesture, she signaled for the branches to be open which formed the entrance to the enclosure. She entered, came close to Jean, and spoke to him slowly in an almost masculine voice. The Portuguese who accompanied her translated: 'I am Princess Zoditu, the Emperor's sister. From now on, you are under my protection', and turning around she walked away taking slow steps. Her women and the Portuguese who revealed himself to be the doctor of the contingent sent by the Portuguese king supported Jean so he could walk. They followed the Princess till her own enclosure erected very close to that of the Emperor. The canvas wall sheltered many tents, the biggest meant for the Princess, the others for the members of her entourage. Jean was brought to one of them and laid down with all possible precautions on a comfortable bed. Princess Zoditu's women undressed him and the doctor examined his wound. It was deep but not grave. Jean had more than anything lost a lot of blood. The doctor put some ointment and bandaged it.

Jean fell into a deep sleep. In the middle of the night, he woke up. Under the light of the lamps he saw huddled in a corner of the tent, a feminine form. An extraordinarily beautiful woman watched him anxiously. She had a very long neck, an elongated head and beautiful almond eyes. Jean recognized her as one of the women following the princess he had noticed. He smiled at her and signaled her to come to him. She jumped up and fled the tent, as gracious as a gazelle. Her long finely-pleated robe accentuated her figure. She had allowed Jean to notice her long tapered thighs, her flat stomach, her breasts placed high. Comforted by this vision, he fell back to sleep with a smile on his lips.

The next morning, Princess Zoditu visited him again but he was too weak to get up. In spite of the heaviness of her features, she was not really ugly. Her powerful features, her tall built, her broad shoulders made her look more like an ogre, but a sensual ogre, capable of arousing desire. Jean began to thank her for saving his life. She purred with satisfaction. Seated at the edge of Jean's bed, she spoke to him at length about Ethiopia and its rulers. She was very proud of the history of her family that merged with that of her country and she enjoyed reminiscing about it.

'It was more than two thousand years ago, the Queen of Sheba, the fabulously beautiful Balkis whose states in Ethiopia consisted of approximately what today is Yemen, having heard of the famous King Solomon like the rest of the world, left for Jerusalem at the head of an endless caravan. She made a grand entry into the kingdom's capital surrounded by extraordinary pomp and luxury. King Solomon waited for her on his gold throne. One look was enough for them to fall madly in love with each other. They shared a blazing passion, the result of which was a son, Menelik. Menelik, who became the ruler of Ethiopia, was Zoditu's first ancestor. Later, the dynastic ties between Ethiopia and the Levant allowed the Christian missionaries to evangelize this corner of Africa, Ethiopia becoming probably the oldest Christian kingdom. Then Islam appeared which conquered the

Levant and North Africa, completely isolating Christian Ethiopia, the memory of which was beginning to disappear from Europeans. However, during the Middle Ages, they began to hear of the famous kingdom of the priest Jean, the pontiff king of an immense Christian empire which no one knew where to find and which led to a number of expeditions, all unsuccessful. On the other hand, the Muslims knew well about the existence of Ethiopia. Now Islam, taking on a new momentum, with the extension of the Ottoman Empire, had decided to put an end to the existence of the Christian Empire.

'One day,' continued Zoditu, 'the Muslims attacked the empire. This was approximately twenty years ago. They came from the north and the south. Their forces seemed irresistible. Worst of all, their greatest general, their most intelligent strategist, was the Sultan of Adal. He was known by his nickname "Grand" the left-handed. My father, Emperor Lebna Dengel, attempted to stand in the way of his advance. Our troops were crushed in complete defeat and my father had to retreat with his army. I was a child then, but I remember our flight, the anxiety, the despair of my father, of my grandmother, and the Empress Eleni. We went from refuge to refuge. I knew fear, for we were afraid to be taken prisoners by the troops of the sultan of Adal. We knew that instead of killing us, he would sell us as slaves. It was the fate suffered by all our fellow compatriots, women, men, children, who fell into their hands. The manuscripts that recount our history, the oldest gospels of Christianity went up in flames. He destroyed the crosses, religious icons, he burnt churches and monasteries, he stole the crowns and the jewels. Fleeing without stop, we reached the frontier of the empire. One more defeat, and we would be hunted out of Ethiopia. But there came a respite, because the Muslims were too far away from their base. My father died of grief, and my brother Galadewos succeeded him immediately after. He was only eighteen years old, but was already of an exceptional caliber: intelligent, energetic, determined and courageous. He rallied whatever was left of our troops and immediately began a counter-attack. He won one, two and then three battles. He progressively pushed back the Muslims and seemed invincible. In a few years, he succeeded in throwing back the invaders out of the empire, and, to crown his victory he killed the sultan of Adal, the "Grand". He had saved Ethiopia. Since then, he has ruled with wisdom and firmness. I assist him as much as I can and I flatter myself for being his most heard adviser. The women, in our dynasty, have always played an important role, because they know what they want and they always get what they want…' she said staring at him. Jean, quivered involuntarily. His face became strained. 'You look tired,' sniggered Zoditu, 'I will come back later.'

The whole day, Jean wondered about the gracious apparition from the previous night and about Princess Zoditu's visit. In the evening, after his supper, he feigned sleep. With half-closed eyelids, he saw the flap of his tent rise and the beautiful follower of the princess entering quietly. He opened his eyes, smiled at her and got up extending his arms to her. This time, she didn't pull back. She sat on his bed, exactly the same place where Princess Zoditu had. Pointing her finger towards herself, she pronounced the name: Tanis. Jean lightly touched her hand, she shuddered with fear. She got up and went to sit on the floor in one corner of the tent. Jean, weak and tired, felt sleep coming over him. She fixed a stare at him that was as full of affection and love as he had ever seen. Deeply moved, he happily fell asleep. All night, she stayed to watch over him. When he woke up, she had disappeared.

The whole day, he dreaded the visit of Princess Zoditu. Fortunately, she refrained from it. He waited impatiently for the evening to come and Tanis to appear. By chance, she arrived early, and as if she had taken an important decision, she lay down on his bed next to him. He took this gesture as the acquiescence of her desire. Slowly and softly, he kissed her, he caressed her. She didn't protest. On the contrary, she cried, she moaned and Jean noticed that she suffered. He used his instinct and his experience to make her experience a pleasure. It took him time. This thrilling game, at times frustrating, became more and more exciting until they together accomplished the satisfaction of their bodies. The night passed, and wearied and satisfied, they were resting side by side, when they heard noises outside the tent. Tanis had just about time to cover herself with her gown and to huddle up in the corner of the tent as Jean had seen her the first time. Princess Zoditu entered. She stood in front of Jean's bed and surveyed his nudity, her eyes burning with desire. She let her richly embroidered cape slip, and she was naked. Her intentions were only too clear. 'You must not, princess,' muttered Jean.

'Anything I want becomes possible.'

'I do not love you, princess.'

'I don't love you either, I just want you as a lover.'

Jean threw a distraught glance at Tanis who hadn't moved. It was then that the princess noticed her. In an instant, she understood it all. She threw herself on Tanis who attempted clumsily to cover her nudity and slapped her so hard that her nails left bloody traces on the unfortunate's face. Tanis didn't let out a cry but fat tears rolled down her cheeks. Then, with powerful force, the princess pulled the young girl as if she were a wisp of hay, and indifferent to her own nudity, dragged her outside towards her own tent. Jean jumped out of his bed, and completely nude himself, went out after them. A hand stopped him. A foreigner, a European, stood in front of him. He recognized the Portuguese uniform. 'What are you doing here? What's going on?' whispered Jean.

'Let me introduce myself. Rodrigo Aveiro at your service.' He was lanky, brown-haired, pale and droopy-eyed. His nonchalant appearance hid the most dreaded sword of the kingdom of Portugal and a mind as sharp as his sword. Jean tried to move him aside. 'I must go to help Tanis.'

'Precisely,' the intruder retorted back in a dragging voice, 'nothing will happen to her as long as you stay away from her.' This argument struck Jean who then calmed down.

'But,' continued the Portuguese, 'it'll be better if we went inside to talk.'

The two men returned to Jean's tent. The latter's curiosity was completely aroused. 'What are you doing at this hour inside Princess Zoditu's enclosed quarter?'

'I watched you when you were sentenced to death. You displayed great courage. I understood that you had not renounced our religion. I have followed your love affairs. Princess Zoditu is a true ogre, she takes men, one after the other, keeps them for as long as she gets pleasure out of them, then disposes of them, but contrary to fairy tales, she does not devour them. Most are known to have had brilliant careers after their liaisons with her. You could imitate them, but I do not think this venture is to your taste.'

'That woman frightens me.'

'Most of all, do not let her see that for she is vindictive, and if you really wish well for this beautiful follower that you call Tanis, then above all abstain from expressing the slightest interest in her.'

'I cannot get over her.'

'I only ask you, for the moment, to be patient. Later, we will decide. While waiting...'

Jean interrupted: 'Why are you looking out for me?'

'That is exactly what I was going to explain to you, but before that, allow me to summarize our history to you. At the beginning of this century, we the Portugese, succeeded in going around Africa, then sent our fleet of ships in the Indian Ocean to establish our trading posts there, spreading our colonial empire more with each passing day. So, the Ethiopians noticed our presence. When the father of the new emperor, Lebna Dengel, defeated by the Muslims, found himself at the edge of final catastrophe, he called us for help. We responded to his distressed call. Debarking on the coast, we climbed till the plateau of inland Ethiopia, and fought for the Ethiopians. A number of us also lost our lives. Becoming indispensable, we planted ourselves in the country. Just as the Ottoman contingent of which you were a part was assigned the task to put order in the anarchic troops of the Muslim princelings, similarly, our mission was to train the Ethiopian armies that were primitive but accustomed to fight. We trained them in modern warfare. We lack intelligent and determined men like yourself. On the other hand, if you accept wearing the Portuguese uniform, you will be protected from the princess's prosecution and the intrigues of the court.'

Jean had endured so much in such little time that, without thinking too much, he accepted the proposition of Rodrigo Aveiro.

'What name did you bear at your birth?'

Jean fell silent for a few seconds, then clearly announced: Soragno.

'Welcome, Captain Soragno, to the army of the King of Portugal, my ruler.'

Hired under the Portuguese banner, Jean soon realized that there was no lack of opportunities for battle. Although Emperor Galadewos had defeated and pushed them back, the Muslims did not cease foraying into the empire, and the imperial army was on its feet going from one front to another to stop them. One morning, he sensed great agitation in the encampment.

'We are leaving for battle,' announced Rodrigo Aveiro.

'So,' asked Jean, 'would the women be sent to the capital.' He had immediately thought that during the war, Princess Zoditu would be keeping her followers in shelter, and that there wouldn't be any time to catch a glimpse of Tanis. Rodrigo smiled: 'In the Ethiopian empire, there is neither a capital nor a palace. It is a nomadic monarchy, which exists where the emperor exists. For centuries,' he explained, 'the dynasty has constantly been moving according to the needs of the administration or the necessities of the war.'

The camp rose rapidly and they set out on march, the emperor on his canopy which almost completely covered him, Princess Zoditu on her litter carried by men on their backs, princes and courtesans in their brocade coats, monks in white draperies, soldiers covered in feline hide of lion or leopard, guards armed with long spears, and semi-nude servants. In spite of the distance, Jean recognized Tanis walking behind the princess's litter. She moved forward with her inimitable walk, marked with elegance and sensuality, head held high, she seemed to be smiling at life, and Jean swore to see her again. He himself was riding with the Portuguese contingent. The glistening procession spread over several kilometres, wound its way over round hills, between rows of huge tress that swayed in the light wind.

At a stopover, the hordes of servants put up the enclosure of the emperor, of the princess and of other dignitaries, then erected the multicoloured tents. Lastly, from big boxes circled with cooper, they took out essential objects of comfort for the royalty, spreading out exquisite carpets, lighting huge bronze chandeliers, arranging small tables encrusted with shell and ivory, putting up pale-coloured gauze curtains with intricate gold embroidery, laying out boxes, ewers, dishes, jade-white or green champagne glasses encrusted with emeralds and rubies. These refined objects of luxury were all imported from

India with which Ethiopia actively traded. Jean had never seen creations as beautiful as these and, due to this bias for poetic luxury, he had his first contact with the fabulous country.

The imperial army flushed out the Muslim troops. The battles began. Muslims were pushed back. A precarious kind of peace returned for a few months. Jean performed audaciously in the battle. His combative and military leadership qualities were noticed and he participated in a number of operations of this dormant war and led the Ethiopians to victory. He proved himself to be more and more popular amongst them, he came across as firm but also tolerant and generous. He was never devoid of the deepest simplicity and he knew how to listen. Despite all that he had suffered, he loved life, he loved people, and people treated him well. Only the attitude of Emperor Galadewos towards him worried him. The King didn't hide his distrust and his repulsion, and yet, not only did Jean show the highest respect for him, but he constantly proved his loyalty and his devotion to him, taking a stand back, attributing the victories to the emperor's wisdom and his experience for which he was himself responsible.

When he mentioned this to Rodrigo, the latter shrugged his shoulders: 'Although you have remained a Christian, you have served in the Egyptian Army. Now, anything that has been touched by the invaders of his country makes him lose all consideration and all rationality. Don't think he loves us for all that. If he had to do without foreigners, he would do so happily, except that, he needs us and does not dare oppose that we attribute more and more important posts to you.' Rodrigo stopped to think for a few seconds. 'Perhaps there is also another thing. Galadewos listens a lot to his sister Zoditu. It is possible that she has filled his ears with the venom that she has accumulated against you.' Jean expressed his skepticism. 'On the contrary, I think she has calmed down and is not bothered about me anymore, she does not see me, she does not notice me, she has forgotten about me. Thank god for that.' Rodrigo had a dubious expression, but said nothing.

Jean didn't tell Rodrigo that he had seen Tanis again in secret. One evening, after her services to Princess Zoditu, she managed to get out of the camp without being noticed and came to Jean's tent. Since then, they met for a few hours at night, whenever she could. Love grew between them, all the more so as their bodies found harmony in desire and sensuality. One night, she explained to him her reluctance in the beginning. During the invasion of Ethiopia, she hadn't had the luck of Princess Zoditu, who managed to escape, and thus be spared.

Raped by the Muslims who had seized her village, she was then sold as a slave and, for many years, she was submitted to the most harassing sort of work, to the erotic whims of men of all age groups. During the re-conquest by Emperor Galadewos, she was freed, but for the longest time she could not think of men without repulsion. Everything changed the evening she saw Jean imprisoned, condemned to death and then saved. She had instantly fallen in love with him, but physically she was still not ready. She had offered herself to him in love but Jean left her to come in her own time and got her to know pleasure. Jean, by his consideration, by his softness, and his affection, had won her over.

Thanks to Tanis, Jean discovered Ethiopia through the eyes of love. He was filled with enthusiasm for the lake Tana which was lined at the end of the horizon by high mountains always covered in snow and whose green banks were an invitation to the travellers for lounging around. On several islands in the middle of the water were monasteries. Others were constructed on rocky plateaus protected by abrupt cliffs, which were accessible only by a rope ladder thrown down by the monks. Jean visited monolithic churches in the form of a cross dug into the rock and were connected by secret passages. The army constituted of the moving force of Ethiopia, sometimes influential, sometimes very weak, whereas the Ethiopian Church was the very axis of the country, irremovable and all-powerful, almost more important than the emperor. Galadewos understood that as well as he leaned over the clergy to reinforce his power.

Jean had become indispensable, and was increasingly absorbed by his military missions. Extraordinarily demanding of her servants, Zoditu rarely let Tanis take a break. This misfortune thus left little time for lovers to experience and live their poor but intense moments of happiness. Time passed, they took less and less precautions, encouraged in this imprudence by the fact that no one seemed to pay attention to them. This continued until the day when Rodrigo Aveiro took his friend aside: 'Be careful of the princess. She notices everything and forgets nothing.'

Jean rebelled, 'I do not see what you are alluding to.'

Rodrigo was irritated at being taken as stupid, which he wasn't: 'Your affair with Tanis has no future. The princess will never grant her freedom. You have already acquired a considerable position for yourself because of your own merits. An even brighter future awaits you, but only if you are careful.'

'I don't feel like being careful, I am free!'

'So you are going to go head-on into difficulties and dangers that you don't understand. Do not take this risk. Go back home, go back to Europe.'

Jean said nothing to that. 'By the way,' Rodrigo started again, 'you never told me where you came from. Do you have a house, a family?'

And so, Jean spoke. He knew he could count on Rodrigo's discretion. Brusquely, he freed himself of the weight that he carried which constituted the secret of his birth and his link with the Commander, by talking about it with his friend. Maintaining his usual nonchalant composure, the Portuguese seemed immensely interested, his dragging voice incessantly posing questions.

'I do not think this could interest you,' he announced to Jean, 'but the King of France died a few years ago.' News from Europe passing through Lisbon reached the Portuguese contingent in Ethiopia… at least six months late. Jean wondered if the death of the son of Louise de Savoie, his enemy, would in any way change things for him. Rodrigo guessed his question: 'His son, now the King Henri II, succeeded him. Apparently, he is a good and generous man. You could return to France and unveil yourself.'

'I have found here the happiness that has escaped me for so many years. I have no intentions of abandoning it.'

'Even if you don't try to retrieve your potential inheritance, wouldn't it be nice to reconnect with the continent of your childhood, your adolescence, and to find again the universe that is yours?'

Jean did not protest, he was absorbed in thinking. The Portuguese pressed his advantage: 'At least try, without definitively cutting yourself off from Ethiopia, and spend a few months in Europe. Go and think about it there and you will find the voice of reason.' The siren-like voice of the ever-composed Portuguese triggered temptation. Just then, as luck would have it, not too far from them, Princess Zoditu's litter passed. Behind, among her escorts, Tanis was walking with her inimitable walk. Jean looked at her, then shook his head. He was not leaving Ethiopia.

Several years passed like this. Jean continuously fought battles and became the most popular general of Ethiopia. He sought out occasions to see Tanis. Their love blossomed clandestinely. Contrary to what Rodrigo had predicted to him, Princess Zoditu noticed nothing.

The sultan of Adal, the terrible 'Grand' who had almost completely destroyed Christian Ethiopia was well and truly dead, killed some ten years ago by Galadewos. However, he had left a widow behind, Wanbara, a Muslim worthy of the personality, energy and the audacity of Christian princesses of Ethiopia, the Queen of Sheba, the Empress Eleni... and Princess Zoditu. From rubble she raised the kingdom of her deceased husband, reconstituted a formidable army, and resumed the attacks against Ethiopia. The confrontations between the Muslims led by Wanbara and the Ethiopians increased. To put an end to it, Galadewos decided on a full-blown war of extermination upon the sultanate of Adal. The Portuguese supported him but Rodrigo Aveiro demanded that Jean command the Ethiopian Army. The Emperor turned a deaf ear to this, he insisted that an Ethiopian general be appointed chief of his troops. The 'ras'[1] Johannes was thus made deputy to Jean. This powerful chief of tribes was tough and capable, but his views were old-fashioned and his strategy outdated. From the beginning, Jean and he clashed over the tactics to follow. The Portuguese officers insisted on adopting that of Jean's, which led the Ethiopian Army to achieve victory after victory. Finally, Jean led the assault on the capital of the Sultana Wanbara, Harar, despite the so-called impenetrable fortifications that she had raised. Her kingdom conquered, Wanbara disappeared. The Emperor had a triumphant entry into Harar. The two generals, the French and the Ethiopian, marched along with their soldiers. The latter, who had lived the unpleasant reality of the war knew exactly what had happened. They acclaimed Jean without paying any attention to Johannes. Galadewos, for whom the conquest of Adal's sultanate represented an undreamed-of success, was stung about the fact that he owed it to a foreigner. His sullen expression on this victorious day spoke of his state of mind.

After the capture of Harar, the imperial horde marched towards the North. It moved around like this for several weeks before it stopped in the middle of a magnificent landscape. Peace returned, Jean had the time to explore the region. He discovered the oldest convents in the empire. They had been plundered by the Muslims, but some of them still conserved treasures that he could study.

One morning, news spread in the encampment that the King had discharged Johannes because he wouldn't pardon him for indirectly being the cause behind Jean's glory. Too strong to be chased out of the court, disgraced, mad with rage, he withdrew to his camp. That night, Tanis did not come to visit Jean, which did not cause him much concern: she could have been held back by the capricious Princess Zoditu. On the second night without her, impatience and anxiety took hold of him. After the third night without any news, he was alarmed, and went to find Rodrigo, always ahead on everything, and asked him if he knew what had happened to Tanis. The Portuguese had no information and seemed hardly interested by the disappearance of the woman: 'Don't be afraid, Jean, she'll come back. Meanwhile, don't think about it…' This last bit of advice burnt his soul. He held back no more, and went to Princess Zoditu's camp and had the courage to stand in front of her.

'Now that is a visit I was not expecting,' she launched at him ironically.

'Where is Tanis?' he roared. The princess did not seem affected by this insolent. Neglecting it, she replied: 'I offered her to Prince Johannes to soothe him in his disgrace.' Jean had enough self-restraint to hold back the insults that he wanted to shout out, but his look at this point was so terrifying that for once, the princess seemed to have lost her confidence. Jean withdrew without saluting her.

Although it was not in his nature, circumstances had taught Jean how to dissimulate. All through the day, he attended to his men he was accustomed to do, under the anxious and sometimes interrogative watch of Rodrigo Aveiro. Neither did he say or do anything to give the latter a reason for worry. That night, he didn't close his eyes even once, and despite his impatience, waited a good part of the night to pass. In the wee hours of the morning, he got up and sneaked into Johannes' camp. Careful about not being seen approaching them, he knocked out the two guards. He entered the tent of the Prince whom he found in bed, with Tanis who lay there apathetic. Before Johannes could call for help Jean had hit him so hard on the head that he heard his skull crack. Tanis, her body frozen as if lifeless, kept her eyes closed. Jean took her in his arms; she opened her eyes and started to cry convulsively. Jean managed to calm her down. She got dressed, and they both left the camp of the 'ras'. They reached the borders of the imperial encampment without being spotted. One of Jean's Ethiopian soldiers was waiting for them there with two horses. Jean paid him generously, then Tanis and him, having mounted their horses, galloped away. The Ethiopian night was luminous enough for them to be able to direct themselves without any lighting.

This brief journey took them to the convent of Abba Salama that Jean had noticed during his promenades. At dawn, they arrived in front of a high featureless wall. An external staircase, so narrow that only one person could climb at a time, took them to the top of the rampart. The monastic building was spread out in a quadrilateral dominated by a type of a donjon on the first floor, which one entered by means of a drawbridge, which was itself quite narrow. Once inside, they were plunged into a mysterious and somewhat oppressive atmosphere. The rooms, the galleries were barely lit by the high and very narrow windows. Smoke clouds rose from incense burners arranged almost everywhere. They crossed monks dressed all in white, silent in their movements like ghosts. There was no furniture apart from mashrabiyahs,[2] behind which they felt some presence.

They reached a room where the abbot, informed of their unexpected arrival, was waiting for them. This man was young and fat, with a carefully trimmed beard, in white clothes elegantly draped and a lot more ample than those of the monks. Acquainted with Jean, at least by reputation, he greeted him courteously but with a certain reluctance. As for Tanis, he didn't even throw a glance at her. Jean knew that a convent could offer them asylum that even the Emperor could not violate. But his intentions had gone further than that. 'You are going to marry us right now, this woman and me,' he declared in tone that brooked no argument. Tanis looked at him with a mix of bemusement and indescribable happiness. The abbot looked a lot less happy. He knew his world and argued that he had to seek the permission of Princess Zoditu for one of her servants to marry. 'You do not need any authorization,' Jean cut him short.

'Perhaps we must wait a bit,' risked the abbot, now more and more suspicious. Jean felt he was losing ground and that his dialectic was not being taken as ecclesiastical, so he turned his argument in the direction which works most efficiently with a good number of clergy on this earth. He took out a pouch of gold coins and extended it to the prelate. The latter announced that the marriage would be celebrated that very hour.

Hand in hand, Jean and Tanis entered the chapel that was on the top floor of the donjon. All along the walls inside were rows of saints and saintesses with large dark eyes underlined with big black lines that seemed to be looking at them with amazement. The mashrabiyahs divided the chapel into two behind which the officials recited prayers. Seated cross-legged against the walls, the monks clothed in white had covered their heads with their shawls, also white, in order to conceal their down-turned faces. Immobile, they looked like strange sculptures. Innumerable candles were lit in over-ornate bronze chandeliers, the flames of which were distinguishable through the thick clouds of incense smoke. The officials following the abbot left through the doors at the centre of the mashrabiyahs. Over their clothes they had put on brocade ornaments in red and gold or blue and gold. In a sullen voice, the abbot recited the customary prayers and proceeded to the demands. Jean proclaimed his responses. Tanis's was only a murmur. The ceremony barely lasted the time it took for the priest to declare them husband and wife. There was no point in congratulations, or in wedding banquets. The newly married retired to the room that was prepared for them in the guest building. They did not need a feast, the festivity was in their hearts.

Next morning, they stayed in their room. Ever since they had known each other, this was the first time they would be with each other, without any time limit, without any obligation to hide themselves. The abbot and the monks did not bother them, and the present was fulfilling enough not to have to create a plan for the future.

At the end of the second day, leaving Tanis behind who was resting, Jean went out to take a few steps in the courtyard. Absent-mindedly he looked at the massive donjon with partially invisible windows, the very high walls that encircled the courtyard in a square and the modest guest-building leaning against one of the walls. The convent of Abba Salama looked a lot like a prison. Jean felt perfectly happy, and yet strange thoughts and irrational worries began to creep inside his mind.

He was immensely surprised to see Rodrigo Aveiro appear in the courtyard heading about twenty Portuguese soldiers. 'You have just come in time to congratulate me, I just got married,' Jean said.

'I know,' Aveiro shot back, without losing his composure.

'How did you know about it?'

'Because your abbot bombarded the Emperor with messages announcing your wedding and asking for instructions.'

'And has the Emperor given them?'

Aveiro abandoned his nonchalant expression and seemed worried. 'Let us go to your room, it will be easier to talk.'

When they entered, Tanis suddenly woke up, and discreetly covered herself with the sheets. Aveiro went up to her, smiled and kissed her hand. Then, with an expression even more worried, he spoke to Jean:

'We have had a very animated morning in the imperial encampment. The counsel took place as always. The Emperor presided over it, with Princess Zoditu on his side. The ministers, all the princes and myself, we were discussing the next military campaign when Prince Johannes burst into the imperial tent. Apparently you had not hit him hard enough on his head to break his skull. Bursting with rage, he went up to Galadewos and in very lewd language, accused him of sending you to assassinate him and steal the woman that Princess Zoditu had offered him. Galadewos, without losing his cool, tried to calm him down but in vain. Johannes was beyond listening to anything. Dagger in hand, he threw himself on the Emperor who managed to dodge the worst but received a deep wound on his arm.

'What followed was indescribable confusion. All the princes and the guards pounced on Johannes and stabbed him. He fell with twenty, thirty stabs, still finding the force to curse the Emperor. When these Ethiopians get down to it, they become complete savages... Only Zoditu remained impassive and very efficiently gave first-aid to her brother. My instinct told me to do as little as possible. Effectively, Zoditu's eyes, full of hatred were fixed on me. In a stentorian voice, she accused you, and your wife, of having armed Johannes's hand. She vomited out all that she had accumulated against you all these years, which, despite my warnings, you had never wanted to see. She said she didn't trust you from the beginning. And you were nothing more than a traitor who's lone aim was power, along with getting Galadewos out of the way, and to put a puppet in his place and hence rule over Ethiopia. Finally, she regretted having saved your life when you were imprisoned. She should have rather let Galadewos behead you, she concluded.

'These were exactly the words what Galadewos wanted to hear. Without hesitation, he believed her. I saw his face harden and take on a ferocious expression. I didn't move, I didn't breathe, I had transformed into a statue, but he saw me and ordered me to promptly leave the tent. I therefore could not hear more. I do not doubt that the Emperor has given the most terrible orders against you and your wife. I have come to warn you. You need to flee this very hour, and I will help.'

Suddenly, the door of the room flew open. Two monks, five monks, then ten monks rushed in, arms raised with long daggers. Some of them attacked Tanis, others Jean. The young woman didn't have the time to react, she was stabbed and fell crying out Jean's name. The latter had the reflexes to get his sword that was hanging on the wall and kill the two monks who were almost upon him. Aveiro took the others from behind. Four monks fell stabbed, and before others returned to surprise them again, the Portuguese pulled Jean out of the room. In the courtyard, the soldiers fought courageously against other monks.

The two men reached the exterior of the monastery followed by the Portuguese soldiers. Aveiro made Jean climb his horse, whipped it to bring it to a gallop, while he and his men having mounted their own started off at high speed. While riding, Aveiro kept checking on Jean who seemed to be neither seeing nor understanding anything, as if he were drugged, and who swung dangerously on his saddle.

One last glimmer of daylight vaguely lit the route. Aveiro did not dare increase speed, fearing that Jean might fall off the horse. They by-passed the imperial camp visible far off, with hundreds of torches lighting the route to the north. It was only after having covered a long distance and riding for many hours that Aveiro ordered a halt; he nevertheless took the precaution of hiding their horses in the bushes and didn't allow the lighting of a fire. He gently helped Jean spread out on the ground. Jean remained immobile in a recumbent state. Without knowing if he was listening to him or even heard him, Aveiro explained: 'Galadewos has always intelligently relied heavily on the Church, the historical pivot, the traditional axis of Ethiopia. Now, in this country, which is often attacked and invaded, the monks are no longer sheep dragged to the slaughterhouse, they are candidates for martyrdom, but after having fought for their skin at a high price. The Muslim invasions led them to pick up arms. Also, it just takes an order from the Emperor for the monks of your convent of Abba Salama to turn into murderers.'

Jean got up, shaking, feverish, he became voluble: 'I will arouse the army, men who I led to victory will follow me. I will overthrow Galadewos. I will imprison him and subject him to the same fate as Tanis.'

'You will do nothing of the sort,' Rodrigo Aveiro replied icily. 'Without the Emperor's support you are nothing for the army. He has probably already learnt that you have escaped again. He is going to do everything in his capacity to find you and kill you. You are going to find shelter in no corner of this empire, not even in the remotest. Believe me, you have only one choice, to leave the country as soon as possible.'

As if to lead him back to sanity, they heard at that very moment riders galloping past on the road, probably the Emperor's guards on their chase. Rodrigo had to use all his force to pull Jean to hide in a bush. Once the riders disappeared into the night, Jean murmured: 'I have lost everything, I have no desire to live... If they come to kill me, I will receive them with solace.'

'Don't be stupid,' Aveiro broke in, 'you are going to do exactly as I tell you to, and I will lead you out of Ethiopia.'

Beneath his nonchalant appearance and despite his sleepy air, the Portuguese had a great influence on Jean, all the more so when he was in an apathetic state. On Aveiro's instructions, they got on their horses and resumed the route to the north. They were ready for unpleasant surprises and, at every village or town Aveiro made them take precautions to escape the guards on the look out for them. To their surprise, they did not meet with any unfortunate encounter, as if their chasers had vanished into thin air. They passed Axoum where Jean showed no interest in the extraordinary obelisks that stood out in the middle of the countryside. They crossed by the extremely old city of Asmara, and turned towards the sea.

That evening, at the stopover, Jean's melancholy took the upper hand. Talking of Tanis's death, he went back to his past: 'Once again, circumstances have taken hold of my destiny, they have destroyed my future, made me a slave to the situation. During the years I spent in this country, I believed myself to be free, but it was just an illusion. I experienced a burning passion, I got to stroke power, I earned a reputation, and all for what? To once again become a runaway, without a homeland, without a family, without any future.' The Portuguese looked at him with his drooping eyes and heard him without responding, well aware that such a tragedy was beyond any consolation.

It took them several weeks to reach the port of Massawa on the Red Sea. An ancient Ethiopian possession, this city, with its constant invasions and incursions, became a sort of a Turko-Portuguese condominium, a haven where all nations could freely trade. The governors appointed by the Ottoman sultan got along perfectly with the representatives of the king of Portugal in order to share the cake. A senior Portuguese officer, Aveiro had his clout. He had decided to send Jean to India, to his Portuguese compatriots who occupied a large part of the west coast. There was not much time to lose, for the emperor's guards were going to reach Massawa, find Jean and reclaim him, which they would not be able to refuse, at the risk of a catastrophic rift between the Ethiopians and the Portuguese. But there was not a single Portuguese ship at the port leaving for India. There was only an Ethiopian slave ship getting ready to lift anchor. Basically, in exchange for the luxury goods that India provided the Ethiopian court, the latter sent slaves, a profitable trade. The Ethiopian captain did not know Jean, and thus accepted taking the Portuguese officer on board who wished to go to India. Aveiro gave Jean a number of letters of recommendation for the local Portuguese authorities. At the moment of their separation, Jean worried about Rodrigo: 'The Emperor won't pardon you for helping me. If you return to the imperial encampment, he will immediately have you arrested.'

Aveiro had an ironic smile: 'The Emperor is cruel but also cunning. He needs me and my men too much to attempt anything of the sort. He'll pretend as if nothing happened and will never talk of you.'

Jean put his hand on Rodrigo's arm: 'Why did you do so much for me?'

'Because, contrary to what you think, your future, far from being finished, is about to begin. I sincerely regret that you are leaving Ethiopia under such circumstances. But you were not meant to spend your life here.'

'If Tanis was alive… '

'You are above all a prince of the Bourbon House. France is calling you, reclaiming you.'

'I am not even sure if I truly am the Commander's son.'

'And I, assure you, amigo meo, that you are a prince, a Bourbon, and the Commander's son.'

Rodrigo, seeing Jean's distress, also added softly: 'While waiting, a mission awaits you in India.' He turned around and went back to the quay. The footbridge of the ship was pulled back and the anchor lifted. The sails inflated and the ship, slowly, moved away from the Ethiopian banks.

1 Prince.
2 Is the Arabic term given to a type of projecting oriel window enclosed with carved wood latticework located on the second storey of a building or higher, often lined with stained glass.

Portuguese India, 1555

Jean was once again in a slave ship, no longer as merchandise but a deluxe passenger. He pitied the chained slaves in the ship's hold and thought of his own experience when he had been subject to the same fate. And yet, his thoughts were elsewhere. They wouldn't leave Tanis. Leaning over the ships's rails for long hours, he saw her come towards him, her walk that had struck him so much since their first meeting. Her cruel death had inflicted on him a wound from which he would never recover.

The Ethiopians secluded in the high plateaus of their continental empire were not known for maritime trade. Ships and men from the sultanate of Oman and Muscat, a small state southeast of the Arabic peninsula, provided more skilled ship builders and more talented sailors. They traded with all of Africa, the Persian Gulf and India. They had invented ships that were light in weight and fast in speed, had studied the winds of the Indian Ocean, and knew that at certain times they blew from east to west and at others from west to east. They had also chosen a time when the wind pushed them towards their destination. They had even put up a chart of currents in order to be even faster. Their knowledge and experience allowed them to escape the predators that infested the Indian Ocean. Jean had the chance of having as captain the most skilled of all, named El Sihidi. He was bringing slaves he would sell to the sultan of Bijapur, and on his return he insured the transport and protection of the pilgrims from Indian Muslim states on their way to Mecca for Haj. His experience wasn't displayed much during Jean's journey for, at several trade-ins, the latter had noticed the ships that were on their hunt. These were Dutch or English pirates who, jealous of honest Portuguese or Ethiopian traders, did all they could to claim their wealth. However, the sailors of the slave ship, neither impressed nor frightened by the danger and galvanized by Captain El Sihidi, raising a sail here, changing course there, eluded their pursuers.

One morning, Jean saw in the horizon a fortress literally emerging out of the sea. Jahira, planted on a rock, was constructed some forty years ago by the Ethiopians and served as a drop-off point in their commercial activities. The slaves that the ship was carrying were made to disembark there. Boats of weaker tonnage shuttled between Jahira and the Indian coast, a distance of two miles. Jean disembarked at the Portuguese post of Alibagh. He presented his letters of introduction to the Portuguese customs officer who inspected all ships that were arriving or departing. He seemed intrigued by the contents of the letters. He finished by saying that he would execute the instructions indicated in these documents. Jean, who was still in his state of apathy since the journey, didn't even ask what these instructions were. Climbing onto a horse, escorted by several Portuguese soldiers, he set out for Bombay, a small place recently acquired by the Portuguese. On the way, he began to show interest in everything that surrounded him. Palm trees swayed gently along the beaches the ends of which he couldn't see. Large waves from the Indian Ocean rolled onto and died on the immaculate sands. Big floral bushes bordered the dazzling green fields. Jean was touched by the beauty of nature. He crossed a swampy region, then followed tongues of sand that advanced into the sea to the tip of Bombay.

There, his escort did not take him to the Portuguese governor's house as he was expecting, but to the Jesuit mission. Low and rather primitive buildings surrounded a miniscule church. The Jesuit Father, José Marilva, who directed the mission received him and took him to his office. It was a very small room, whitewashed, where the only ornament was a wooden cross, but the shelves were bent under the weight of books and manuscripts. The Father took his time reading Rodrigo Aveiro's letter concerning Jean.

During this time, Jean was able to scrutinize him. Tall, thin, a bony structure, blue eyes, straight nose, a slightly heavy jaw, slightly long teeth, he could nevertheless have been very handsome, except for a detail that Jean noticed immediately: with oily hair and a shiny cassock, there was something dirty about him.

Father Marilva finished reading the letter, carefully folded it and said: 'I have already heard of you. One hears quite a bit about you, all very flattering. It is also said that you could be of illustrious origin, maybe even princely or royal.' Jean's response to it all was just a shrug of shoulders, indifferent, despondent. Father Marilva noticed that straight away: 'You seem low. If you so wish, I could hear you in the confession, otherwise I could quite simply hear you out, I am here for that.'

These simple words led to a stream of words from Jean. Although the Jesuit didn't establish complete confidence in him, he had such a weight on his heart that he felt a desperate need to confide in him. He recounted the tortuous and adventurous path that took him to Ethiopia. He described his meeting with Tanis, the burning desire that they shared, the intense years full of action and, what he believed to be happiness, his marriage to her, and then the assassination of his beloved.

'I have nothing left,' he repeated at the end of his confession.

'Indeed, replied the Jesuit, I feel that your soul rests on a very thin thread in life. Does even a bit of your Christian faith still exists inside you?'

Jean made a non-committal gesture...

'For if the flame of the faith is not entirely extinguished in you,' the Jesuit continued, 'then God's service awaits you.'

Suddenly Jean seemed interested: 'You want me to take holy orders? After all this, why not. Perhaps this way I can find peace in my soul that has till now eluded me.'

The Jesuit let out a dry laugh. 'I don't think you were made for priesthood ... nor for celibacy. You can serve God in a manner that suits your nature. I invite you to contribute to the evangelism of this part of the world, a task that our army and our Jesuit brothers have undertaken.' Jean expressed no enthusiasm but agreed. 'Now remains the question of your name. Rodrigo Aveiro wrote to me that you are a Bourbon prince, the Commander's son.'

'I am not sure of my identity.'

'In any case, a very big name will trouble my compatriots. To serve in our forces, choose one that is convenient to you.'

'I will be Captain Soragno,' Jean replied without hesitation.

❧

The west of India belonged to the sultan of Gujarat and other less important kings. They passed their time making war. Sometimes they called the Portuguese to their aid, while at other times they attacked their trading posts. For two years, Jean participated in these local conflicts. Action returned the taste for life to him, just as India held him back from the depths of despair. This country indeed offered so many images, smells, colours, movements, so much incessant swarming that this extraordinary kaleidoscope prevented him from giving himself up to introspection or sinking into sadness.

Yet he was not satisfied and he expressed this to Father Marilva during a leave that brought him back to Bombay. With his yellow teeth and oily hair, the Jesuit still looked dirty, but his spirit was alive.

'You deceived me, Father,' Jean attacked. 'You spoke to me about evangelizing the pagans, Hindus or Muslims. But the campaigns in which I took part had only one aim, that of spreading the colonial empire of Portugal, and your Jesuit brothers, to my knowledge, are busy more with trading than with baptizing.'

Father Marilva had an ironic smile on his lips and didn't argue. 'I see that what I chose for you has not suited you. Let me think, I will find something else for you.'

One week later, Jean was appointed governor of a beautiful and picturesque province, Goa. Obviously, the Jesuits had a lot of influence in the Portuguese colonies. Arriving at his new post, Jean got down to his job straightaway. A few decades earlier, the Portuguese had annexed Goa, but, in a hurry to spread their empire northwards, they didn't concentrate on consolidating this possession. All that remained to be done now. Jean transformed into a builder, building a vast church and schools, opening up roads and creating a fort, as the

Portuguese authorities required. He made himself an administrator, organizing justice, education, and public order. He made himself an economist, modernizing agriculture and commerce. He became popular amongst the Portuguese who boasted about his qualities. Also, colonists from Portugal were flooding in. He also managed to be liked by the natives, who appreciated him as the Ethiopians had for his tolerance, his firmness, and also his justice, honesty and his open mindedness. Though successful, he remained inexorably lonely. As for Father Marilva, Jean remained slightly wary of him, thus preventing any friendship between them. In the evenings, when he had time to himself, he went out of the city and went for walks on the never-ending beaches with the frothy water touching his feet. He looked at the Indian Ocean with the sun setting into the horizon. He reflected, he analyzed and became sure he was bored.

He went to look for Father Marilva in Bombay. 'I have decided. I want to return to my country, France.'

The Jesuit didn't seem flustered: 'You have achieved brilliant success here. My compatriots and even the Indians are full of praise for you. By your qualities, by the example that you have set, you attract natives towards Christianity as well if not better than our missionaries. You have become the beacon of our presence in India.'

'In Ethiopia, I lost everything when Tanis died. Here, I have gained nothing. I want to go to France to reclaim the inheritance that was stolen from me.'

'Are you actually the son of the Commander of Bourbon? Don't you doubt that?'

A dangerous light lit Jean's eyes: 'Your doubts, Father, clear mine.'

This insolence, instead of enraging Father Marilva, mellowed him, and he continued in a softer tone: 'Portuguese India does not suit you, I shall attend to that. And yet, I would like you to accept one last mission.'

'Where are you thinking of sending me?'

'Instead of leaving for the West, you will leave first for the East, for Hindustan, the heart of India...

'About a century ago, an Afghan chief named Babur, leading his invincible troops, had torn down the mountains, invaded the Indian plains, overthrown the sultans, the kings, the maharajas, the nawabs who ruled the country and set up an empire that covered north and central India. He claimed descent from Tamerlane, perhaps rightfully, that which conferred a sort of legitimacy to him. Also, as a souvenir of this fabulous ancestor, he took on the name the Great Mughal.

'Today,' Father Marilva continued, 'his grandson Akbar is the one who reins, an extremely interesting person, who has just pulled a masterstroke. For many years, he had a prime minister called Bairam Khan who, he believed, took too many liberties and didn't listen to him enough. He asked his general-in-chief and foster brother Adham Khan to organize a coup d'etat against the prime minister. This was done and the prime minister was duly dismissed and dispatched on a pilgrimage to Mecca on the way to which he was assassinated. Quite naturally, the Great Mughal offered the post of prime minister to Adham Khan, but the latter, in his turn, behaved in too free a fashion. He lacked respect for Akbar, and ordered massacres and plundering, which perturbed Akbar. Worse still, furious with the nomination of a minister, he went to the office of the newly nominated and assassinated him. Akbar exploded with anger. Adham Khan, weapon in hand, went in pursuit of his master all the way to his harem with the intention of killing him. What followed was a hand-to-hand clash in the course of which Akbar ended by throwing him out of the window. Adham Khan fell in the courtyard but did not die. Akbar ordered that he be picked up and brought back to the harem and he threw him again from the same window, and this time the minister did not survive. A strong man, one could say of the Great Mughal: a small detail, he has hardly just turned eighteen …

'In fact, Bairam Khan, the prime minister who was sent off, was his regent. From now on, everyone understood that Akbar ruled alone. He is also open to new ideas, curious about everything. From our modest mission in Agra, his capital, we have learnt that he has asked our Christian priests to instruct him about our religion. You will go offer your services to Akbar. He will accept them, as he needs men of experience like you. You will serve God by fueling his curiosity about our religion and by encouraging him to welcome our priests.'

'And by what miracle, Father, will I succeed in presenting myself in front of the Great Mughal?'

'You will accompany me. The Jesuit priests have put together for him a Bible in four languages and in six volumes richly illustrated with miniature paintings. I have been given the responsibility of carrying it. But I would prefer it if you didn't appear to be a member of our mission: your chances of success will be better if you seem independent. I would be happy to take you till the throne of the Great Mughal. After that, you are on your own. It is my last proposition to you. If you fail, if you are not satisfied, if you are not convinced, then that will mean that providence does not wish your presence in the Orient. Then, not only will I let you go to France but also I will ask our Jesuit brothers to help you in your journey.'

'On this condition alone, I accept,' Jean replied.

Father Marilva with dozens of his Jesuits, under the protection of Jean and twenty of his Portuguese soldiers set out for Agra. They went through the interiors of the Indian continent. They went by Solapur, Ahmadnagar, Burhanpur; they went around the ancient holy town of Omkareshwar and reached Bhopal. The journey was not tiring, the routes more or less safe and the company quite pleasant. Jean, in a certain manner, began understanding Father Marilva, or rather his formidable erudition. He had apparently read everything and not only theology but also history, geography, sacred literature as much as profane. He shared his knowledge with intelligence and sensibility. He knew how to fascinate Jean who held on to his every word, and little by little the latter saw his inexplicable suspicions that he had conserved for the Jesuit faith. If they remained strongly reserved in their conduct, intellectually they felt more and more close.

North of Bhopal, they entered a wild desert region that later came to be called Bundelkhand. A dense savannah grew on red and sandy land with deep ravines sunk in them indistinguishable from afar. Travellers who knew what to make of it knew that this region sheltered two mortal dangers, tigers and dacoits – the latter were self-proclaimed bandits of honour, who in reality killed anyone who fell into their hands. No local ruler, not even the Great Mughal, had managed to neutralize them. Helped by the dense and thorny vegetation, and knowing the area like the backs of their hands, they existed without being detected and were never caught.

One evening, the mission camped in an abandoned fort called Shergar. The crumbling fortification encircled a miserable village. Contrary to the usual, the villagers proved semi-hostile towards the travellers. Thanks to their interpreters, they learnt that a band of dacoits had spread terror in the surrounding areas, and the villagers feared that the presence of the travellers, supposedly rich, would only attract the bandits and thus misfortune. Instead of removing the camp, Jean, agreeing with Father Marilva, decided to defend the village.

Bedtime came; the villagers had slept a long time ago, the men of the mission retired to their tents, or rather feigned to retire so that the dacoits would believe them to be asleep. In fact, Jean had positioned all fit men, villagers, soldiers and even Jesuits behind carefully-chosen shelters. Everyone was armed to the teeth and on the alert. Despite these precautions, no one saw the dacoits approach. Suddenly, without any warning, they poured into the village and the encampment screaming, weapons in hand. Immediately, they were caught between the shots of the Portuguese and the villagers who rushed out with their scythes, their pikes and their daggers. Very soon the dacoits were massacred. Very few survived to disappear into the bushes, but most of the wounded left bloody traces behind them for the villagers to follow. Victory was complete.

Next morning, the village chief thanked the Portuguese. He was loaded with meager gifts that were provided by his community. 'Thanks to you, he said to the Portuguese, we shall have shelter for a long time now, for the dacoits won't dare attack us again.' Then, he turned towards Jean and added: 'Shergar will never forget you.'

The mission resumed its way towards north. After Gwalior, the road became broader and busier. Elephants, camels, carts multiplied, as well as travellers on foot. Everyone was heading towards Agra. Soon Jean could make out the rose granite walls of the capital of the Great Mughal. Five years had passed since his arrival in Goa.

Hindustan, 1560

Jean discovered that Agra was a city in the midst of construction. Akbar, the Great Mughal had decided that the old capital of India, Delhi, was too exposed to invasions. He chose the site of an ancient city that was collapsing as the one to build his new capital, on the banks of Yamuna, the holy river. The whole city was nothing more than a builder's yard flocked by innumerable workers who came looking for work, explorers, merchants and soldiers of fortune. From morning till evening, one heard the rolling of chariots carrying heavy stones, one was deafened by the hammering of carpenters, the packed roads were ruled by an incessant commotion. One could barely walk in the alleys of bazaars where unfinished boutiques were open. Jean and his travel companions had to traverse the entire city to get to the other side, because the Portuguese mission was set up outside the walls, the Muslim clergy had prohibited representatives of another religion to settle inside the city. The building for the mission was modest but clean and airy, surrounded by unsanitary shacks of an immense suburb that spread further everyday.

Finally, the day came when the Great Mughal attended a weekly public audience. Jean dressed carefully in European clothes sold by the Portuguese in Goa: doublet, chausses, ankle boots and a feathered hat. He noticed with amusement that Father Marilva had washed himself and looked clean. With their entourage, they headed towards the Agra Fort. There as well, everything was under construction: Akbar was building new ramparts over those of the medieval fortress. Inside, they were building barracks, mosques and residences for the nobles of the royal court. A bazaar held by women was already open, exclusively for the women of the harem. After having crossed several courtyards, they arrived at a vast area carpeted with sand in the middle of which ran cobbled alleys in white marble. A cramped crowd was already waiting there. Father Marilva, without hesitation, went through it to get his people to the first row.

In front of them stood the Diwan-e-Aam, the hall for public audience. Raised by 1.5 metres on a marble base, it was a very big open pavilion. Marble columns also supported a vast domed ceiling. The columns were incrusted with semi-precious stones, amethysts, corallines, jaspers, lapis lazuli and topazes that outlined branches, flowers and birds. The domes were wallpapered with gold sheets. On the façade of the pavilion stood the imperial throne, a sort of a daybed resting on four legs with a stepladder in front. On top was a canopy chiseled in precious metals sparkling with diamonds. In the centre, at the end of a gold chain hung the biggest emerald of the world.

Suddenly trumpets were blowing and drums were beating and everyone froze. The Great Mughal arrived and quickly took his place on the throne, while members of his court and his entourage seated themselves according to protocol. At the foot of the throne on the precious stepladder sat the secretary of the king surrounded by many scribes responsible for writing down the decisions that he would be taking. Immediately the parade of the Great Mughal's favourite animals began, his elephants with their howdahs in gold and silver. Then followed the king's mounts, horses richly caparisoned in gems. After that came the dogs and the falcons for the hunt.

The end of the parade marked the beginning of the public audience. The Great Mughal's secretary consulted a list then gave an order to officers grouped below the marble railing. Each one went looking for a person amongst the imperial audience. The first were the local rulers, nawabs or rajas, then the generals and the ministers. Each one stood at the bottom of the throne describing more or less at length the subject of his request. Akbar listened carefully and dictated a decision to his secretary.

Then came the turn of Father Marilva. He came forward at a firm pace, followed by his Jesuits carrying the six volumes of the Bible meant for the king. In a strong voice, he spoke fluently in Persian, the language of the court. The Great Mughal seemed to take pleasure in receiving the volumes that were offered to him. The nobles, who surrounded him, took them from the hands of the Jesuits, and then the fine fathers retook their place.

Jean wondered how could he approach the king. He understood that he had to be registered in the secretary's list. But, he didn't know anyone in Agra, and Father Marilva had made it very clear that in public they wouldn't acknowledge each other. Jean, to his amazement, saw Akbar's secretary give an order and an officer pulled away to come look for him. He followed him to the bottom of the throne. Immediately a man appeared next to him, very tall and handsome, visibly non-Asian.

He was the interpreter of the court who Jean would learn later was an Armenian. 'What is your name?' began the Great Mughal.

'Jean de Bourbon, Prince of the French blood.'

Jean had screamed out this response so loudly that no one understood, except Father Marilva. After the interpreter had translated it, the Great Mughal smiled.

'So, you must be a rich and a powerful man.'

'On the contrary, Sire, I am a runaway, banished and condemned.'

'What do you ask of me?'

'To enter in your service.'

Jean could not particularly make out the Great Mughal because the gems on his clothes, on his turban, on his throne, on his courtiers reflected such sparkle from the sun's rays that they outshone the people present there. The latter whispered some words in the secretary's ear who gave an order to be interpreted. 'You,' he said to Jean, 'are invited to the private hearing that will follow.' Jean took his place and the hearing continued for hours during which Akbar not even for a moment seemed wearied or inattentive. Then the stream of solicitors petered out, Akbar got up from the throne and disappeared as fast as he had appeared. Officers of the service led the privileged people who had been invited to the private hearing.

When Akbar came up to Jean, the Armenian interpreter too appeared at his side. The courtiers surrounded them. Akbar asked Jean to narrate his story. The latter protested: 'Sire, it is very long, I am afraid I might bore Your Majesty.'

Akbar, on the other hand, asked him to leave out not a single detail. Effectively, when, after several episodes, Jean attempted to abridge the story, Akbar interrupted to ask him many questions. Akbar heard him out with intensity, stinging him with his piercing eyes. He ended with the possibility that he could be the son of the Commander of Bourbon, the biggest traitor in the history of France whose story he had sketched out. When he had finished, Akbar remained silent for a while and then spoke: 'You had asked to enter my service, I accept. How do you wish to serve me?'

'Give me the cannons, Sire, they are the only friends I have had all my life.'

The Great Mughal smiled: 'You are going to be the great master of my artillery.' Jean could not hide his amazement. 'Isn't that too much, Sire? You do not even know me well.'

'I know my men. You are certainly a prince and also an honest man.'

In the evening, he found Father Marilva again in the mission of Jesuits. He seemed irritated and asked him bluntly, 'Why did you introduce yourself as a Bourbon?'

'Because I am a Bourbon.'

'But you are not certain!'

Jean smiled: 'Since I have been mature enough to think, I have wondered who I am. Later, Father Soragno put me on the track, left me to think that I was the son of the Commander of Bourbon. He believed in that, but he had no proof. Thus, for years, the dilemma has been eating away at me. I was no one, and in that case, I was free and did not owe anything to anyone. But if I was the son of the Commander, in that case, didn't I have the right to show myself worthy of the valorous warrior, so as to defend his memory? I faltered from one possibility to another, until something, very slowly, established my conviction. These were the sentiments of those who have mattered in my life and who directed me in the course of my life, the maternal affection of Dona Carmela, the solicitude of Father Soragno, the loyalty of the sergeant of Aurigni, the passion of Latifa, the interest of Dawood Pasha, the love of Tanis, the friendship of Rodrigo Aveiro, but also the devotion of my soldiers, Egyptians, Ethiopians and Portuguese. The confidence that you showed in me gave me confidence in myself. Confidence in my destiny, confidence in my identity. All of it has convinced me that I am the noble descendant of a very illustrious family. Having come to know the Commander by hearsay, I have understood that he would not have done all that he had for me, if I were not his legitimate son. By coming of age and after the experience that I have had, I feel more tested, stronger and more thoughtful. The need to solve the mystery behind my birth has weakened. And, paradoxically, my certainty has strengthened. Finally, and above all, I have my instinct. I know, without a doubt, that I am the son of the Commander. And yet, I had not yet decided to assume my identity. And then I was introduced to Akbar. The piercing look of this young man was fixed upon me. I knew it was of no use to try and deceive him, but above everything I had the desire to tell him, the first one, the truth.'

What followed was a long silence during which the two men remained lost in their thoughts. Suddenly, Jean asked the priest: 'By what miracle did the Great Mughal's secretary know of my existence?' Father Marilva smiled sarcastically: 'I have several contacts in the king's entourage. His interpreter, Krikor, the Armenian, is very close to me. He has the ear of the Great Mughal's secretary. It was easy for me to slip your name in.'

Stretched out on his bed, unable to sleep, Jean went through the day in his head again. Even though life had taught him to be careful, to take his time to examine every aspect, to take wise decisions, he felt an instant enthusiasm towards Akbar that surprised him. Akbar had immediately succeeded in moving him. Hitting his forties, when he couldn't see where life was leading him, suddenly the doors to a future opened in front of him, a future which included this young man with an exceptional destiny, capable of evoking irresistible élans, and who was in dire need of men who were experienced and loyal. In a second, Jean had decided to devote his life to Akbar, for whom he felt a strange kind of affection. He fell asleep, for the first time in months if not years, peacefully. From now on, he had a cause whose name was Akbar.

The next day, Jean settled himself in the Agra Fort, in one of the palaces for the nobles of the court, which was not entirely completed. He found, at a little distance from the city, old warehouses that had been transformed into arsenals. He started by repairing old cannons, then putting up a foundry to create new ones. He worked flat out to endow the Great Mughal with artillery that was worthy of his might. He was given two interlocutors in the court. First was the Armenian interpreter, Krikor Izpenian. This tall and handsome boy with black hair, big dark eyes, became his friend. After all, weren't these two the only Christians in the Great Mughal's court? Krikor followed with interest Jean's work and interrogated him at length on the subject. Krikor was a friend of the Great Mughal's secretary who became one of Jean's too. Zair Khan was too tall for an Asian, with very high cheekbones, elongated eyes whose pupils were in constant movement, a bit like the eyes of a chameleon. Nonchalant, insolent, he was completely devoted to Akbar who depended a lot on him. Jean knew that the viziers, the ministers changed but only the secretaries lasted. Also, he used the services of Zair Khan to get money from Akbar for the workers and bronze for the cannons. Moreover, he could directly ask Akbar since the latter often visited his arsenal. Not only did the Great Mughal very closely follow the creation of his artillery, but the criticism that he voiced over the form of one or the range of another were also pertinent.

During his visits, the Great Mughal came very simply dressed. Much as he covered himself with jewels during the ceremonies of the court, the rest of the time he appreciated sobriety. On white cotton pants, he put on a chemise that was particular of that era, made of several layers of white muslin. His turban was adorned with a modest sarpech.[1] Each time Jean would be surprised by the banality of this man's traits, whom he had already come to consider a genie. Nothing remarkable, nothing majestic, and yet Akbar possessed a natural authority, on top of being a manifold man. He was very young, as was evident from his face, and yet, eventually, Jean noticed how it didn't possess a juvenile expression. He was born old. One could tell from his face that Akbar bore an enormous weight of responsibility since his birth. Jean discovered that the king was already learned in multiple crafts and showed that he was gifted in many fields: he was a remarkable shooter, he knew how to domesticate wild horses, which he loved to ride, he showed talent in woodwork, as a gunsmith, as a blacksmith. He was also knowledgeable in medicine, knew bloodletting and had hence saved more than one life. Above all he was an untiring worker, who had understood the necessity of establishing a strong state before starting wars. Also as a priority, he was involved with the administration where he promulgated reform after reform and with the army, which he was determined to modernize. He also got along marvelously with Jean on this subject and appreciated his expertise in work.

To express his satisfaction, he invited him as often as possible to the court. When his cannons let him some free time, he would go to the Agra Fort to assist in the durbar, the public audience. He also participated in the council, which brought together the ministers and the vakils. He accompanied Akbar when he went hunting. He played in his team of choka, the Indian polo.

In the evenings, he attended parties that Akbar gave in his private apartments. Jean no longer required an interpreter. In a few months he had learnt the official language of the court, Persian. Akbar spoke gladly of his young past to Jean. Jean had learnt of the ordeals that he had to go through but he loved listening to Akbar describe them. The latter repeated: 'Like you, I have also had a turbulent childhood, perilous.' His father, the Great Mughal Humayun, was dethroned by an usurper, Sher Shah. He not only lost his throne but also had to flee India. He was reduced to begging for assistance from the neighbouring kingdoms and he barely received the means to feed his children. Akbar remembered those days when he had known hunger, anxiety and fear.

Then the situation reversed. Humayun reconquered his throne. He had barely regained supreme power when he died of a stupid accident. He had fallen from the ladder of his library and broke his neck. Akbar succeeded him at the age of twelve. He had to suffer humiliation at the hands of the adults who took advantage of his young age to bully him, he had seen his regents, his ministers put the state through regulated breakdowns, do what they thought was best without asking his opinion or following his advice. Years passed by, the titular Great Mughal was treated as someone insignificant and everyday he felt his impatience grow to knock them over.

Jean got more and more attached to this young man whom the whole world envied and whose life had been anything but enviable. Jean admired him for coming out of his hardships without resentment or bitterness.

Jean had not forgotten the mission he had been charged with by Father Marilva. Whenever he had the change and when he thought the moment to be right, he would slip in information in the Great Mughal's ears about the Jesuits, who promised eternal salvation even to the condemned and took care of the most destitute. He succeeded in such a way that soon Akbar announced his plan to visit the Portuguese mission. He left with great pomp from the fort. His elephant wore a brocade caparison with a gold howdah on which he was seated along with Jean, while behind him a servant sheltered him from the sun with an enormous parasol with pearl fringes. Dozens of elephants carrying members of the court followed, surrounded by guards on their feet, in sparkling uniforms, spears in hand.

The arrival of the procession put the miserable suburb, where the mission was situated, upside down. The habitants crowded to hail the king who responded by smiling and graciously waving his fly swat with a gold handle encrusted with rubies.

Father Marilva, surrounded by other Jesuits, waited at the door of the mission. Akbar visited everywhere, got explanations for everything, asking as was his habit a hundred questions. In the miniscule chapel, he fell short in front of an incredibly beautiful painting of the Virgin Mary painted in Italy that the Jesuits had carried from Portugal. He was narrated the story of the God's Mother. In front of his courtiers who stood cramped in small rooms, he announced to Father Marilva that he wished to have many Christians and many churches in his empire, like the Ottoman sultan does, because 'Christians are workers, honest, discreet.' Father Marilva, who saw himself at the crown of his career, could not hold back his joy. Later, he frequented the palace on invitation to explain the Christian faith to Akbar. He sometimes engaged in these with a lack of tactfulness, which irritated Jean, a witness to these meetings. The Jesuit first took up the king's weaknesses. He reproached his abusive consumptions of bhang, liquor with an opium base, and of arak. The Great Mughal did not sometimes mind getting drunk. To the Jesuit's reproaches, he contented himself with a smile and by turning a deaf ear.

When the Jesuits spoke to him about paradise, Akbar replied that Muslims also had one where one found the best food, the most exquisite drink and where one could make love to the most beautiful women in the world. Father Marilva retorted that this description was completely false and that paradise was the opposite of that, a place of purity and virtue.

Another time, he directly attacked Akbar by saying that the Prophet Mohammed was arrogant. Jean admired Akbar for controlling his anger. 'Our Christ,' continued the Jesuit, 'never boasted about himself, it was the apostles who recounted his miracles, whereas in your Koran, Mohammed himself brags about his own miracles, which one cannot verify.' The mullahs and the good Muslims of the court trembled at his declarations, but Akbar kept his calm, and demanded the same from the others. Even better, he showed his favour towards the Jesuits by offering them European food that one of his chefs was responsible for preparing. So the Jesuits devoured roasted chicken, vol-au-vent and tarts.

Father Marilva from now on believed himself to have all liberties and became overzealous. At every meeting he was invited to by Akbar, he demanded the edification of churches, schools and monasteries. He demanded that an ever-increasing number of Jesuits be allowed to settle in India. The Great Mughal started spacing out his invitations, and Jean was irritated to see the Jesuit lose, by his own fault, the ground that he had contributed to set for him. He attempted to put some sense into him. The only result of it was that Father Marilva multiplied his demands for a hearing and hassled Jean to intervene in his favour.

Akbar got his revenge by teasing the Jesuit. One day, he summoned him and took him to the courtyard where a huge pyre was burning. Next to it stood a Muslim monk... 'This mullah,' said the Great Mughal, 'is ready to throw himself into the fire for our faith, are you ready, Father, to go to that extent for yours?' For once, Father Marilva seemed discomforted and Jean had to hold back a smile. The Jesuit grumbled: 'If I throw myself in this fire, that would be committing suicide, which our religion strictly forbids.'

The Great Mughal usually awoke early. Every day, before the clock struck seven, Jean and the closest collaborators of the king found themselves in the waiting room of his private apartments. One morning, Jean was surprised to see Father Marilva there. The latter, just as surprised, had been summoned by a messenger of the court. Akbar came, as always, very simply dressed. He took the whole lot across the courtyards of the palace until the ramparts that towered over the sacred river, Yamuna. Below, on the large banks, which spread out to the edge of the walls, a big crowd had already gathered. In the middle was a funeral pyre, raised high, on which was spread out the body of a man, sumptuously attired. He was a noble from the court who had died the day before. A cortege appeared and made its way through the crowd. The Brahmins who endlessly repeated the word 'Ram' stood around a very young girl dressed in a red and gold sari wearing magnificent jewels. She moved forward like a robot and Jean thought that she had been drugged. On reaching the pyre, the Brahmins helped her climb it. She then lay down next to the body of her husband. She was practicing sati, a Hindu custom according to which a widow sacrifices her life at the death of her husband. The Brahmins lit the pyre. A cloud of smoke rose, enveloping the dead body and the young girl. Father Marilva broke his silence to protest vehemently:

'If this young girl has been forced into this sacrifice, then it is a crime. If she is doing it voluntarily, then it is a suicide. Both are vigorously condemned in our religion!'

'Islam, my religion, does not regard sati well, but you asked me to be tolerant towards your religion and to allow its practices. I did so. Right now you want me to condemn the same tolerance towards the religion that is the most widespread in my empire and to prohibit its practices.'

'There is only one religion, that of the living God Jesus Christ,' grumbled the Jesuit, while Akbar smiled ironically.

Jean at this point was horrified, and he couldn't help looking at the pyre. Jean understood that Akbar was not only testing the Jesuit but also him. Father Marilva was right in condemning the sati, and Akbar was right in authorizing it. Two worlds, two cultures were confronting one another. Instead of detesting India, Jean realized that he had a lot to learn and understand about this fascinating and enigmatic country.

The same evening, he received a laconic note from Father Marilva, pleading him to come see him that very hour. Surprised, curious, he rushed to the mission. The Jesuit was waiting for him with blazing eyes, pursed lips, and hair dirtier than ever glued to the skull. He barely opened his mouth to spit out his words: 'You don't support me anymore in front of the king. You have forgotten your mission. I ask myself if you have also forgotten your faith!' Before Jean could reply, he was showered with a torrent of reproaches, making him insinuating, perfidious, insulting, corrosive. 'Perhaps the lure of gains is irresistible for you, you shall indeed gain a lot from this crowned pagan. Life must be pleasant alongside him. It seems there is nothing he refuses himself and thus he shall refuse nothing to his favourites.'

Jean wanted to remain patient. He knew that if he complained to the Jesuit about his lack of tactfulness or his disastrous insistences, it would only worsen the situation. 'You are mistaken, Father, it is true that I am happy to serve Akbar and, no matter what you think, I try to move forward our cause as much as I can.'

'I must therefore conclude that you have lost all credibility alongside the Great Mughal and that he has become a fanatic Muslim like those who, in the past centuries, have disgraced history.'

'Akbar is an open and a tolerant person, but he hates being jostled. One must take one's time with him.'

Father Marilva went red: 'Choose who you serve, God or Akbar?' Jean didn't reply, which hurt Father Marilva even more: 'You are nothing but ungrateful, you have forgotten all that I have done for you, you have forgotten that it was I who introduced you to the Great Mughal…'

'To better serve your interests before those of God,' Jean couldn't help retorting.

The Jesuit turned crimson with rage: 'A renegade, that is what you are. All that remains for you to do is to become officially Muslim to flatter your master.'

'God will judge me better than you, Father.' And before Marilva could retaliate, Jean withdrew. He knew he had just made a dangerous enemy for life.

❧

Akbar, the Great Mughal's empire progressed and prospered. And yet, there were always the Rajputs, a warrior race that had for centuries occupied the northwest part of India. The Rajputs were famous for their courage, their fighting spirit and their heroism. Fiercely independent, rebellious to all authority, they were proving difficult to integrate in the Mughal Empire. Peace with them remained precarious; their rajas always seemed ready to pick up arms against the Mughals. The chief of the Rajput clan was the Maharaja of Marwar, Uday Singh. Akbar's grandfather, Babur, in a battle, had killed Uday Singh's grandfather. And this didn't help improve things between the two men. However, on Akbar's demand, he had agreed to send his eldest son, Prince Sanga, to his court as hostage. Although he was treated as a privileged guest, he wasn't thrilled by it. He hated the Mughals and was also scared of them. Jean was taken by pity for this young man, lonely and withdrawn, who had been taken a prisoner. In the year 1565, tension rose between the Rajputs and the Mughals.

One evening, Akbar invited Prince Sanga, as he often did, to one of his private parties. Having drunk more than necessary, he asked the young Rajput if he would be loyal to the Great Mughal or his father, in case of a conflict. Jean saw Sanga go pale and lower his head without responding.

The next morning, while Akbar was holding his private counsel in the presence of Jean, the officer responsible for watching over Prince Sanga came announcing that the latter had disappeared. In all probability, he had escaped during the night. 'This means war!' roared Akbar. And immediately he exploded against Uday Singh and his Rajputs: 'For months they have been secretly preparing to attack me, they have been stacking up weapons, getting their troops together, they urge their men to fight and die rather than subject themselves to my rule.'

Jean had never seen Akbar, always so self-controlled, in such a state. 'They want war, they shall have it,' he screamed, 'but it will not be a war like the others, it will be jihad,' which means holy war of Islam against Hinduism. Jean shuddered at this announcement that belied the tolerance that until now Akbar maintained towards Hinduism. But on second thoughts, Jean realized that Akbar's anger was nothing but an act. Prince Sanga's flight was only a pretext. In fact, Akbar had decided to put an end to the Rajput resistance, latent or not, for once and for all. The sole purpose of jihad, the holy war, was to motivate the troops. It was in the name of Allah that one fought the Rajputs to subjugate them better. After spending five years besides Akbar, Jean had learnt to comprehend his ruses and his drives.

As for him, the great master of artillery, he was finally ready. His friends, the cannons, were in perfect condition and only waited to be put to use.

One fine morning, the gigantic army – comprising a hundred thousand men – set out on the road. For weeks, it moved without meeting the enemy. Sometimes they crossed bristling expanses of abrupt hills, sometimes cultivated plains, sometimes thick forests where the trees had the biggest leaves that Jean had ever seen, and which were home to a number of felines. The peasants were first terrorized by this enormous concentration of men who marched in front of their eyes, but once they saw that this army bought their products from them instead of demanding them, they were reassured. The rajas whose states they passed through either escaped or submitted hastily.

One day, in the middle of a hilly plain, Jean saw an impressive plateau rise which ran a mile and a half and was protected by cliffs with 200-metre-high peaks. The apparently very thick ramparts ran all along the summits. It was Chittor, the capital of the Rajputs and the objective of Akbar. His army had barely arrived at the bottom of the cliff when his spies informed him that Uday Singh, the maharaja of Marwar, the chief of the Rajputs, had deserted Chittor. His general staff had convinced him that the place was not impregnable and that he risked falling into the hands of the Mughals as a prisoner. He thus took off to another fortress that was even more inaccessible and better defended. He left in Chittor five thousand men with women and children.

Akbar had meanwhile decided to take this symbol of Rajput independence. He spent a month establishing siege there. His troops started by destroying the region and hunting down inhabitants so as to avoid being taken from behind. A huge pit was dug all around the Chittor plateau to shelter the troops positioned to attack. Jean, after the detailed reconnaissance, set up three positions from where he would bombard the ramparts.

On the big day and on the order of Akbar, they launched into action. The cannons launched by Jean's men seriously burst through the fortifications. The trumpets rang in the attack alarm. The infantrymen rushed in but despite the enormous disproportion between the two armies, they were pushed back. Indeed, Chittor could only be reached by a narrow banister that climbed to the formidable gate. The troops suffered huge losses and Akbar had to announce a retreat.

The next day, the atmosphere was morose in the war council. It was practically impossible to attack Chittor. Also, though the cannons had made holes in the ramparts, they had not destroyed them. The siege could last months if not years. And hence Jean proposed another tactic: the sappers were to dig mines under the Chittor plateau which, on exploding, would cause the collapse of one part of the cliff as well as the ramparts that stood upon it. In addition, he would cast a cannon on the spot, only one, but one a lot more powerful that those the imperial army currently owned. This cannon was meant to destroy the entrance gate of the fortress and its thick defense towers, thus allowing the sappers to enter. Akbar approved the plan and work started on it immediately.

Jean took fifty-eight days to get the mines dug by the sappers in the places that he had chosen and to smelt the biggest cannon that India had ever seen.

On the fifty-ninth day, everything was ready. At dawn, the imperial army was ready for war. The sappers awaited only a sign from Jean to light the wick of the mines. Jean stood next to the gigantic cannon. Akbar came personally to join them. The besieged became suspicious that something out of the ordinary was happening for, from the telescope, one could make out them holding on to the ramparts. The Great Mughal gave Jean permission to commence. The sappers lit the wicks of the mines that ran along the dug tunnels under the Chittor plateau. A second after, such a violent explosion took place that even the most sturdy of soldiers received a jolt.

But instead of the entire section of the cliff and ramparts collapsing, it shattered the enormous rocks which were stacked at the bottom of the cliff and which fell on the trenches full of infantrymen, dug in for the siege. A complete silence followed the explosions. And then clouds of smoke and dust rose up in the air, along with cries of pain. The rocky area had killed three hundred soldiers and wounded hundreds of others.

Jean was speechless with shock and horror. The besieged immediately understood what had just happened and noisily expressed their joy from the top of the ramparts. Akbar's rage turned towards Jean: 'How could you commit such an error, you clumsy cursed soul,' he shouted. The insult stung Jean: 'I never commit errors!' Generals and senior officers didn't dare utter a word. The silence was broken by a mellifluous voice: 'Then, there has been an act of treachery.' It was Krikor, the interpreter and friend of Jean's who spoke. 'It could only have been an act of treachery…' murmured Jean without assessing the consequences of his affirmation. The Great Mughal spoke to Jean in a sharp tone: 'You were responsible for positioning the mines. You are under arrest in your tent until this affair clears up,' then he withdrew with the members of his general staff. Not one amongst them dared stay beside Jean, the disgraced one. The guards, following the lead of an officer, took him to his tent.

Hours passed while he wondered what could have happened. He had at length studied the position of these mines, had calculated their range. An accident like the one that had just taken place, according to his estimations, was inconceivable. It had thus been an act of treachery, but by whom? For what? Upon thinking about the king, whose trust he had just lost, despair seized him. He thought he saw the unlucky star under which he had been born gleam more sinisterly than ever. Cursed he was, cursed he would remain. Suddenly, he saw the flap of his tent rise silently. In came Zair Khan, Akbar's secretary. He was seized by élan. 'No,' the visitor interrupted him, 'I have not come on behalf of our master. I have simply come to extend company to you as you are my friend.' He was carrying a huge flask of wine. 'To cheer you up – he sniffed – despair always smells bad.'

Then, informally, he lit the incense burner, adjusted his body over a multitude of cushions, and swallowed a big gulp of alcohol. 'Obviously there is something strange happening. I did my research. The mines were not placed where you had ordered them to be.'

'But who has transgressed my instructions?'

'Some of your officers.'

'They didn't really act on their own initiative?'

'That I could not find out. But in any case, the mines were placed in a manner so as to provoke the accident. On the other hand, Krikor, the interpreter of the court, who you believe to be your friend, accuses you in front of the king of perfidy; he is affirming that you allowed yourself to be bought over by the Rajputs and that you did all that to sabotage the siege.'

Then along with the dry and dark humour which was characteristic of him, he recounted a thousand anecdotes, repeated a number of rumours from the court, attempted racy jokes which made Jean laugh and relaxed him. At the same time, he thought about the revelations by Zair Khan. While listening to him, he took a paper and started to draw. Zair Khan, whose verbal stream had slowed down, started to yawn. 'So, it is time for us to sleep. We will see what tomorrow brings to you.' Jean extended to him the drawing that he had completed. 'Here is the exact plan of the mines as they should have been positioned and as they must be positioned in the tunnels that I had dug. Give this to the king. He should order the following of my plan, and if my mines do not do their job, and if they provoke another accident, then I must be executed. On the other hand, I ask the favour of aiming the Grand Cannon myself. An officer will stand by me, and if I don't achieve my target, once again, I must be beheaded straight away. Finally, ask the king to allow me to participate in the assault. An officer will follow me who, if the slightest of my gesture hints at suspicion, will be responsible for shooting me.' Still yawning, Zair Khan agreed and withdrew.

The next morning Zair Khan presented him Jean's requests. Akbar granted the first two but refused the third. The mines were placed following his sketch very precisely. The Great Cannon was placed even closer to the fortress, covered under the trench. Akbar let Jean give the signal. The mines exploded all at one time, and the explosion was even more powerful than the last one. The besieged and the besiegers remained shaken for a few seconds.

This time, the mines did their job. A considerable part of the cliff collapsed, sweeping along a big piece of the ramparts and the defenders. Immediately, the Great Cannon entered into action, and pointed by Jean, shattered the towers and the bastions of the fortress gate. The shot was so powerful that the imperial army could see the Rajputs literally fly in air and fall back torn in pieces. Akbar then gave the orders for the general assault. Jean was constrained to remain in his place. He saw the infantrymen rush the entrance ramp and under the firings of the besieged enter the fortress. Akbar was amongst the first row of assailants. With one musket shot he succeeded in shooting down the commanding Rajput of the place. The morale of the besieged was strongly affected but not crushed: they resisted with all their valiance. The battle lasted the whole day and it was only at nightfall that Akbar gave the orders to retreat. He wanted to avoid a useless and bloody battle in the dark. In any case, the Rajputs didn't have the time to repair their walls during the night as a lot of them had been killed. A second assault the next morning was enough to take Chittor, which no longer had any strong defense. On returning to the imperial camp, everyone was exhausted to the extent that they could think of nothing but rest.

Only the next morning, Akbar remembered on waking up, that he had not taken any decision about Jean. The hour of attack dependant on him, he knew the take over would pose no difficulties and if carried out promptly, would lead to a rapid victory. He thus had time. He summoned Jean and his accuser, Krikor, the interpreter, to his tent. His tent, in fact, was a complete house made out of fabric. The outside was a thick canvas painted in bright colours, the inside was full of embroidered silk, velvet in all colours, the inner walls also in precious materials demarcating different rooms, the king's bedroom, the council room, the ablution room and the reception room. The doors were made of muslin with delicate motifs embroidered on them. Precious carpets covered the floor, low sofas spread with pink and silver brocade ran along the walls. Low tables made out of precious wood supported huge silver chandeliers.

In the presence of Jean, Krikor, whom he had believed to be a friend, repeated his accusations. The Master of Artillery had betrayed and had deliberately sabotaged the first attack by provoking a serious accident. Jean was so disgusted that he didn't even try to defend himself. Akbar, listening carefully, was distrustful of everyone. 'It is evident that the aspects are against you,' he said to Jean, 'but,' he added turning towards the interpreter, 'for what reason would he betray?'

'For money, of course.'

'That, I cannot believe,' Akbar said straight from his heart. 'We can perhaps accuse Captain Firangi of everything, but not of dishonesty.'

Krikor replied, 'Your Majesty has been fooled like many others. Me, myself, in my humble position, have been.'

'What proof enlightened you on that?'

'In fact, Your Majesty, it was the reverend Father Marilva, the chief of the Jesuits, who opened my eyes. He warned me against the one you have trusted, he painted the true picture to me and recounted a lot of episodes of his life that prove his hypocrisy. Moreover, the reverend Father had paid doubly for learning the truth since he was one of the victims of this Master of the Artillery's betrayals.'

While Krikor spoke, suddenly the truth dawned upon Jean: It was thus the Jesuit who was behind his misfortune. He had not forgiven him for not implementing his orders. He had therefore built this entire operation leading to the fatal accident with the lone intention of incriminating Jean. As he confided in him not so long ago, the number of his contacts in the court were many and he could have easily corrupted directly or indirectly many of Jean's officers, who were probably already spying for him. By denouncing the Master of the Artillery through the interpreter, his own creation, he made himself look good, since he didn't hesitate sacrificing a Christian like himself to protect the Great Mughal even more. The latter was shaken but not entirely. The accusations of the Jesuit that were passed on to him by Krikor disturbed him. On the other hand, he could not accept being deceived by Jean to this extent. Perplexed, irritated, he grumbled: 'Perhaps I should make you both torture each other to get to the truth.'

At that very moment, a terrible racket exploded in the imperial camp. Alarm calls, charging of muskets, 'Alert! Alert! Take arms!' came from all directions. In a few seconds, the noise moved dangerously close to the imperial tent. 'The Rajputs are attacking us.' Swords slit through the canvas that was the wall of Akbar's room. Jean had already leapt up. He snatched a sword from one of the guards, rushed outside and began to fight against a horde of attackers who had thrown themselves on the Great Mughal's tent. He knew he had to hold them back till the guards came to his rescue. Akbar joined him without even taking the trouble of putting on his armour. He fought beside Jean like an ordinary soldier. Jean received several wounds while defending him but none of them were grave. While Akbar and Jean courageously faced the attackers, Krikor had disappeared.

Soon, the infantrymen and the officers rushed in to free their king.

The Rajputs, instead of waiting for the final assault, had chosen to make a desperate exit. The fight continued for a long time but now it was won in advance. Even though the Rajputs were a few thousand, they fought one against twenty, against thirty. After many hours of fierce fighting, the survivors – there were still hundreds – found themselves surrounded by thousands of soldiers. Akbar offered to let them surrender with honour. As response, the Rajput riders, swords in hand, charged the imperial infantrymen. They attacked them with the most insane courage, and fought till the end, allowing themselves to be massacred to the very last one. Not one of them wanted to surrender or retreat. All of them were dressed in saffron colour and wore their most precious jewels. 'Jauhar...' Akbar murmured while looking at their corpses. Jauhar was the tradition of collective suicide for the Rajputs, accepting it with joy instead of falling into the hands of the enemy.

Akbar intensely scrutinized the walls of Chittor. No noise, no movement, the fortress seemed frozen, apart from the gigantic cloud of black smoke that was rising from the remains of the ramparts. Akbar climbed his horse and asked Jean to accompany him. Followed by his general staff, he climbed the entrance ramp. He found the doors bristling with ironwork wide open. Chittor was a dead city. Not a single living being was found. Colossal pyres burnt on crossroads. They had thrown all the city's wealth into it, carpets, precious fabrics, furniture, coffers, jewels, gems so that nothing could fall into the hands of the invaders. The women of the city brought their young children and jumped into the fire and let themselves be burnt alive rather than become prisoners of the Mughals. Later, Akbar learnt that fourteen maharanis, seventy-five princesses, one-thousand-and-seven hundred women and children had self-immolated themselves. Akbar surveyed this debris for a long time, as he surveyed from atop the ramparts the innumerous corpses, all of them dressed in saffron, which were scattered on the plain like monstrous flowers. 'It felt like,' Jean couldn't help murmur, 'that thousands of suns were falling on us when they attacked us.' Akbar did not reply. Turning the bridle of his horse, with a contorted face, tight lipped, looking straight in front of him, he left the cursed city without a word.

Returning to the imperial camp, he gathered his troops to congratulate them. He went up to Jean and in a strong voice spoke to him: 'Jean, Prince of Bourbon, I thank you for your invaluable contribution in our victory. I had never doubted you.' Jean couldn't help but smile, for Akbar had definitely doubted him, but doubt is a privilege of great kings... 'However,' the Great Mughal continued, 'to reward your precious services, I appoint you Raja of Shergar and Marwar.' Shergar? Wasn't that the fortress in ruins where seven years ago, on his way to Agra, Jean had fought the dacoits who attacked the villagers? 'Shergar will never forget you,' the chief of their community had said to him then. Shergar had not forgotten him since, for now he was the ruler of the small state.

Krikor, the interpreter, was found and brought chained. Akbar ordered for him to be tortured. He confirmed Jean's suspicions: it was Father Marilva who had sabotaged Jean's plan that led to the terrible accident. The culprits were punished, but there were also innocent victims. Akbar did not yet have the power to go against Mughal custom and could not prevent his troops from systematically destroy Chittor or massacre the villagers of the region accused of helping the besieged. The fall of Chittor marked the end of Rajput resistance. From now on, there remained no one to contest the Great Mughal's authority in the whole of North and West India.

Akbar had taken a vow that if he won the war against the Rajputs, he would go on a pilgrimage to Ajmer, one of the most venerated places for Islam in India. On reaching the venerable and magnificent city, he duly offered his prayers in the shrine of Moin-ud-din Chisti, his favourite saint. His visit coincided with the month of Ramzan. Several times during the day, he returned to the shrine to say his prayers. He took advantage of this to offer sumptuous presents to the poor and the pious. Jean, who had followed him in his journey, accompanied him to the door of the shrine. Being a Christian, he was forbidden to cross the threshold. But from afar he saw the king, draped like a good Muslim in a white cloth that served as a shroud, take a number of rounds of the saint's tomb. He thought again about the events that had just taken place. He could not forget that Akbar had indeed doubted him. He blamed him for not having done anything to prevent the massacre of the Rajputs. He wondered if Akbar was as admirable as he had believed him to be.

When the latter left the shrine, Jean went up to him: 'Has Your Majesty also prayed for being victorious in the next holy war that he will be waging?' Akbar instantly caught the hidden resentment in the question. He responded to Jean in a high and intelligible voice that could be heard by his entire entourage: 'I came here to thank Allah for helping me win this war, but I have also taken another vow. There will never again be religious wars in my reign. I want that all religions of the universe be not only tolerated in my empire, but also welcomed, that their incumbents freely display their dogma and that they practice side by side.' Jean was looking at this young man of twenty-five years who talked in a revolutionary voice of tolerance and of liberty. Won over instantaneously again, he felt as moved as he had during their first meeting.

Barely returned to Agra, Akbar began his search for Father Marilva who it seemed, had vanished into thin air. Jean didn't have any difficulty convincing Akbar to spare the other members of the mission, innocent of the crime committed by their superior and who comprised valuable men. However, instead of giving priority to Christians, the Great Mughal called for priests from other religions as well. And thus Brahmins met Jains whom they had considered until now as heretics, the rabbis got to know Zoroastrians, representatives of the ancient religion of the sun, Sunnis greeted Shiaites, Muslims like themselves but awful schismatics in their eyes. Evening after evening, Akbar gathered them on a terrace in his palace. Seated comfortably on brocade sofas, feet stretched on thick layers of Isfahan carpets, catered with exquisite food and the most delicious fruit juices. They discussed under the presidency of the king. The latter held the principle that there was only one god in the universe, the same in all religions. He asked the believers of these religions to agree amongst themselves on the dogmas that link all the religions. The discussions often got out of hand over ferocious debates. Akbar would thus leave the priests, ordering them to reach an agreement until dawn and went and joined his close friends for private parties where not just fruit juice was served. Invariably there would be agreement, but this did not discourage Akbar, who always hoped to reach a syncretism of all religions and receive the blessings of the unique god.

But this broadness of mind was not shared by the entire world. One fine day, a respected priest of the empire, Mullah Mohammed Yazi, issued a fatwa, a Muslim condemnation against the Great Mughal, according to which the latter was so isolated from Islam that all other true believers were justified in raising arms against him. The result was instantaneous. In the east of India, Bengal had entered into a state of rebellion, so had the neighbouring province of Bihar. The rebels had massacred the viceroy appointed by Akbar. Throughout the country, the ulemas fearing for their own privileges spoke against the king and outdid one another in spreading the rumours that the king was disregarding Islam and getting closer to Christianity. Even in Agra,

Akbar's popularity had visibly declined. In a few weeks, the young victorious emperor, idolized by his subjects, had become an enemy of his own religion. For Jean, the tension was palpable even in the court. Akbar distanced himself from Christianity. He limited his visits to the Jesuits, delayed sanctioning the construction of a church. However, he continued to rely on Jean. Jean advised him to be firm, because letting go of the policy of tolerance would be interpreted as weakness and thus become an advantage to the enemies of the throne.

In the east, the revolt was spreading. Akbar wanted desperately to rush there and set the rebels right, but he didn't dare leave Agra. He had found out that one of his brothers, who probably supported the revolt secretly, was waiting for him to leave so he could attempt taking over the throne. Akbar was more determined than ever, but under these circumstances he could do little. He simply had to hold on. How and for how long was the question now. In any case, it was now that he needed more than ever, the support, the advice, the friendship and also the firmness of Jean.

One morning, Jean could not get up: he felt weak and feverish. He made a huge effort to leave his bed but he fell. He had vomiting and diarrhea. The personal doctor of Akbar came rushing in, informed by his servants. The fever was rising. Jean could neither eat nor drink. The worried doctor gave him some potions, which seemed to worsen his pain instead of easing it. Over the next few days, his condition deteriorated even more. He was still unable to eat and his fever remained very high. His heart was beating almost ready to burst, at other times his pulse was almost non-existent. Akbar, who was continuously informed about his condition, came to visit but Jean didn't even recognize him. He had become unconscious. He knew he was going to die. Images, memories, faces appeared in his head at these hours when it was no more night or day for him, being neither awake nor asleep. Father Soragno, Dona Carmela, the sergent of Aurigni, Tanis, these deceased had been stolen from him, all seemed joyful, ready to welcome him to their world.

At the end of a week, closer to death than to recovery, he felt a pleasant physical sensation: a cool soft hand was caressing his forehead. Then the same hand delicately lifted his head. He was made to drink some liquid with an unpleasant taste. His condition was so serious that he hadn't even realized that the same procedure had been taking place for the last few days. He felt slightly better, he felt he could stand on his feet again. However, his condition was such that he continued to remain inert.

One morning, two days later, he was able to open his eyes a little. He saw bent down over him a face of a European woman. He couldn't keep his eyes open and fell back into an unconscious state. However, he felt that he was being made to swallow once again the nauseating liquid. Little by little, very slowly, he started recovering. He regained his lucidity, though he was so exhausted that he was incapable of even lifting his hand. The European woman fed him like a child. He recognized his servants who had not left his bedside. He recognized Akbar who came everyday for an update on his condition, but he was in no position to say anything, he could not talk, he only managed to blink his eyes as a sign of recognition.

Soon, he was able to make out clearly the woman who was taking care of him. She had a handsome face with strong features, big hazelnut eyes, a slightly large nose, sensual lips, dusky olive skin, round cheeks and light brown hair. Every time Jean progressed a little, she had a huge smile and even her eyes smiled. She was dressed in Indian clothes. Even though the patient was incapable of responding to her, she spoke to him to motivate him and regain his forces, recover his energy, his optimism. She expressed herself in French but with an accent that he was not able to place. He didn't know what medicines she was giving him, but he knew by instinct that it was she who had pulled him from the clutches of death. The first words that he said her were thank you, then, immediately after he asked her who she was. 'My name is Julia Mascarehnas, I am a Portuguese and I am the doctor of the imperial harem.' Jean was not in any state to be surprised by that or to wonder by what miracle a European woman had studied medicine and had been added to the Great Mughal's harem, as a physician. Soon though, he was able to articulate the question that had been in his mind: Why was Akbar's doctor removed, who had taken care of him in the beginning, and Julia's services called for? The Portuguese's face hardened, she looked quite embarrassed and then spoke softly: 'It is better to ask the king himself. It was he who hurried me to your bedside.'

At the time of his first meeting with Akbar, Jean asked him the same question. 'Why Julia?' There was a long silence. Akbar then spoke in such a soft and steady voice that it sometimes made him incomprehensible: 'You were poisoned, Jean. The rebels who revolted against my power in the East, the mullahs who hate me because I want to limit their shameful privileges, the devious who, like my father, only wait for the day when they can stab me behind my back, all my enemies have targeted you. You are my best adviser and most heard out one, and since you are a Christian, my detractors are convinced that it is you who is pushing me, not only to favour Christianity but also become a Christian. Thus, it is you who has to be eliminated and it is by using the sacred name of Allah that they have taken on a criminal job by the most powerful, most efficient of allies: my mother, Hamida Begum. You know, like the rest of the world, how I love and respect her. You know there is no wish that she has expressed that I have not granted. And yet, recently, without informing you, as I didn't want you hurt, I had to oppose her by refusing firmly to what she had asked. She had in fact asked me that the Bibles brought by the Portuguese monks be tied around the neck of a donkey and taken around the entire city. When I refused, she retorted back saying that the Portuguese had tied the Koran around a dog's neck and then exhibited it throughout the city of Ormuz. It doesn't suit, I explained to her, a great king to reply to evil with evil in this respect, for the matter of all religion, is the matter of God, and I cannot avenge myself on an innocent book.

'Hurt very profoundly by my refusal, that too the very first one for her, my adversaries directed her rage against you. They made her believe that there would be no salvation for the real religion as long as you were beside me. The moment I learnt about it, I knew you were in grave danger, for not a single person in my court disobeys her instructions, well aware of her privileged position. Who poisoned you? On whose orders? I don't want to know. But because I was not completely sure about my doctors, I called for Julia. First of all, she is an excellent practitioner, perhaps the best that we have, for as a woman she relies more on her instinct than her knowledge. Finally, being a European, she would be intent on healing a brother from the same race.'

Jean worried about the situation. It was now a few months since he had been incapable of following the situation, or even thinking about it. Akbar reassured him: the advice that he had given Jean to simply hold on for as long as possible turned out to be excellent. He had held back and had won. An army force sent to Bengal and Bihar had reestablished order, not without difficulty, but in an expeditious manner that suppressed even the vague will to rebel for a long time. In the court, the schemers and the conspirators were discreetly dispersed or completely eliminated. Akbar's brother who had conspired with the rebels against him had been sent off to the most occidental province of the empire and was appointed the viceroy of Kabul, a post that was largely honorary as he was under constant surveillance. The mullahs had calmed down and Akbar was able to resume his informal meetings with the representatives of all faiths. As for the mother, Hamida Begum, she had implicitly realized that Jean was the most loyal, and the best assistance of her son. Without owning up to her involvement in Jean's poisoning and without anyone ever knowing the truth, she was publicly cheerful over his recovery.

Jean was recovering, but gradually. Julia continued to come everyday for his treatment. He was intrigued, if not to say attracted by this woman, so gentle and yet so efficient, so straightforward and yet so reserved. Jean refused to admit that she intimidated him somewhat as she always remained her own master, without showing signs of weakness, without really trying. One day he gathered the courage to ask how she had arrived in Akbar's harem. Without hesitating, Julia started her narrative.

'My sister Maria and I, we belong to a minor Portuguese nobility. Born in Lisbon, we lost our parents when we both were very young and thereafter grew up in an orphanage founded by our King Jean III for girls in the same situation as us. Each girl in the orphanage had to pick a profession to pursue in life. I chose medicine, which, as you know, is not a profession for women. However, they respected my wish, and I received education from the best professors in my country. The orphans, on reaching an adult age, were sent off to Goa to be married in

Portuguese India to men from the royal military or the royal administration. But the pirates, who had heard about these freighters, were watching. They managed to stop these ships and sold my compatriots to different Asian kings. They were European, they were white and they fetched very high prices. These pirates were all Muslims: there were amongst them some good Christians like the Dutch corsairs who took over the galleons on which we travelled to Goa. They were bringing the lot of girls of which we were a part to Surat and sold my sister and me there. The Great Mughal has agents in all the important ports on the Indian coast. These agents bought my sister who was so much more beautiful than me, but they also included me in the lot so that we wouldn't be separated. We were brought to Agra and presented to the Great Mughal. He was immediately attracted to my sister, and made her a part of his harem. As for me, having learnt that I had studied medicine, he appointed me as the ladies doctor.'

Jean asked if Maria was not too unhappy, forced to become one of the many beauties who garnished the Great Mughal's harem. 'Maria unhappy! On the contrary, she is very happy. The king honoured her by marrying her, and she could also practice her religion. She is known in the harem as Akbar's Christian wife. He lets her pray in front of our holy images, he encourages her to read the gospels, and he has even decorated her apartments with Christian symbols.'

Jean worried about Julia's future. The Great Mughal often offered one of the women from his harem to victorious generals, to governors of provinces he wanted to honour, to princes whom he wanted to ally himself with. In fact, Julia risked ending up with a man who was a lot less tolerant and gentlemanly than Akbar. Julia burst out laughing, 'I am neither young enough nor beautiful enough to become a prestigious gift, and then the king really needs my medical services.'

Jean was touched to see Julia underestimate herself. She was just barely in her thirties, not only was she young but also extraordinarily bright and attractive. Jean found her pretty. There was something in her that made her personality shine.

On her part, she allowed herself to be seduced by Jean. This dark-haired giant, with almond-shaped blue eyes, strong, energetic, and a natural commander, who she had seen reduced to helplessness, had overwhelmed her. Despite his fifty years of age, he maintained the youthfulness of body but above all of mind giving him the appearance and the reactions of a young man. His face, only lightly wrinkled, maintained his strong features. Exercise had prevented his shoulders from slouching. The years had passed without grazing his roughly sculpted beauty.

Jean was surprised at how easily Julia could get out of the imperial harem, a world which was hermetically closed, populated with women and eunuchs, where no man could ever enter and from which no information ever leaked. A proof of this was the fact that Jean, in spite of his proximity to Akbar, had never heard about the Christian wife. 'I stay in the harem,' Julia explained to him, 'but neither am I a wife nor a concubine of the Great Mughal, I am not, literally speaking, a part of it. Also I am authorized to leave the harem but only for reasons that are specifically connected to my medical knowledge and for a limited time. Therefore, once you are healed, I will not have the right to visit or even see you... '

Immediately, Jean's face took on a gloomy expression. Julia, realizing what she had just said, also had an expression of deep sadness. It was the idea of not seeing each other that made him and her discover the emotion that from now linked the two of them. Although he was far from the passion he had felt for Tanis, without realizing it, he had became closer to Julia, to the point of falling in love with her. The sadness he saw on her face as she announced their imminent separation only proved that his sentiment was shared.

Little by little, though still very weak, Jean started to resume his daily activities. He once again assisted at the durbar of the Great Mughal and his most private meetings. Julia was always on his mind. Finally, he gathered courage and opened up to Akbar. He confessed to Akbar what he felt for the doctor of the harem. The Great Mughal had one of his charming smiles that conquered all those who came in contact with him, and immediately announced that he gave him Julia as a wife. On being informed, she was ecstatic with joy. Jean felt happier than he had ever been.

The ceremony took place in the Portuguese mission. A Jesuit married them in a small chapel built inside the building. The next day,

Akbar declared Julia as the 'imperial sister' since Maria was considered the empress of India. 'There is no better way of expressing my friendship with you than to make you my brother-in-law,' the emperor said to Jean. In order to thank god for having allowed them to unite and for saving Jean's life, they received the authorization from Akbar to build a tiny, modest church, which was a grand first in the imperial capital. Beside the mission's chapel, reserved for the Jesuits, there had never been before a Christian sanctuary inside the capital of the Mughal Empire.

Marriage put an end to Jean's long convalescence. Barely married, barely recovered, he was sent off by the Great Mughal to war. Firstly against the Afghans, who were more rebellious than before. Jean succeeded in besieging and winning the city of Kandahar at the end of a few hours of cannon firing. Then he went to pacify, in the southwest of the empire, the wild nomadic tribes and thus added vast territories to those already owned by Akbar.

Meanwhile, Julia gave him two sons, Saviel, and the second who Jean named after the Commander of Bourbon, Charles. However, the Great Mughal was constantly calling for his services, and was sending him almost everywhere, refusing to realize that his best lieutenant, already over fifty years of age, was beginning to lose his vigour. Jean once took the initiative and asked him for leave to go and explore the principality of Shergar and Marwar that Akbar had offered him and which he had not had the time to visit.

He left to go and stay there for an indefinite time with his wife, his children and his servants. His properties constituted of vast stretches of a particularly wild region. A thorny savannah alternated with red sand sunk with deep ravines. He started to rid his states of their two traditional predators, the tigers, and also the dacoits, bandits who for centuries now had scoured the province and prevented it from developing. Security hence returned. Jean worked towards improving and developing agriculture. He thus inaugurated the beginning of prosperity.

Upon his arrival in Marwar, not unlike in Shergar, he found only two vast half-abandoned forts to live in. He got palaces built there, not too large but comfortable, airy and brightly lit, and he added chapels. Just and charitable rulers, Jean and Julia soon became popular. They appreciated the fact that their sons were growing up far from the unhealthy atmosphere of the court and came in contact with the harsh realities of everyday life, at the same time learning nature's secrets, and taking advantage of the freedom offered by this wild and magnificent countryside.

At the end of the hard day, he climbed the ramparts; he surveyed the vast expanse of land – peasants returning from the fields, silence settling in with the light dimming. All this made him nostalgic. He took out the pouch of gun powder of the Commander of Bourbon that he always carried and looked at it for a long time. He thought about France, his country, which he had never known but had heard about so often. He imagined splendid castles, enchanting gardens that had been described to him by Father Soragno, Rodrigo Aveiro and other Europeans that he had met in the course of his life. The marvellous estates could have been his. Recognized in his titles, he saw himself living there with his wife and children. This picture that he created was more appealing than a rustic 'palace' and unproductive savannahs. All of it was nothing more than a dream but perhaps it was not impossible to transform it into reality.

However, the Great Mughal could not resign himself to being separated from his first lieutenant and best friend. Finally accepting that he could no longer send him to the far ends of the country, he tricked him into coming back. One day, a messenger brought a farman from the king appointing Jean the superintendent of the palace. This appointment was a massive sign of trust, but it also meant an enormous responsibility. From now on, the entire life of the court would be depending on him. Even though the price to pay was heavy, Julia and Jean were not unhappy to come back to the nerve-centre of the empire. They hence came back as a family close to the Great Mughal. Akbar had abandoned Agra and moved the new capital to Fatehpur Sikri, which he had just completed: an enormous city in pink granite stood where, not long ago, was an expanse of fields. Along with Julia, they climbed large steps at the top of which stood monumental gates. Behind them was a large space where mosques and opulent palaces were lined. Further away, buildings arranged in a checkerboard pattern, elegantly decorated sheltered all departments of administration of the empire. Fatehpur Sikri was as much a pleasure home for the Great Mughal as his work place. In this inspiring setting, reforms were made under the direction of Akbar, which would modernize the empire.

Hardly had they settled in the huge apartments that Akbar had given them that Julia rushed to the harem to see her sister Maria, the only one amongst his wives and his innumerous concubines, that Akbar truly considered his woman. Jean never met her, no man was allowed to see the women of the harem, but he benefited from a trip into the countryside with these women under the watch of eunuchs, and Julia gave him a visit to her apartments. He noticed immediately the cross on top of the doors, the frescos representing Annunciation and other Christian symbols that Akbar had put on display in Maria's home to express his respect towards her religion.

Once in Fatehpur Sikri, Jean was at once drowned in work. He missed working with arms where his atavism pushed him, but he also developed a taste for his new tasks. He had a lot on his hands to ensure the functioning of a court as large as this one, but above all, even if he didn't move from his offices, each day had risk and the unforeseen awaiting him. His taste for action, his sense of order and also his talent for improvization were constantly put to the test, so much so that Akbar incessantly asked for his advice on everything.

In the year 1590, the court was moved back to Agra where it remained in the palace-fort that stood on the banks of the Yamuna. During this time, an embassy of the king of Portugal, led by the count of Minas visited Agra. Jean had seen the Portuguese at work: insatiable imperialists, they had conquered the west of India, but Akbar's authority was so strong that he did not fear their annexations anymore. The development of commercial relations with Europe could only be an advantage to the empire. Jean explained these reasons to the Great Mughal, who agreed to receive the ambassador. For the occasion, he displayed all the splendour, all the luxury that his court was capable of to impress the visitors. The gathering took place in the Diwan-i-Khas, the room for private audience. The courtiers, all men, gathered there in their fine clothes and jewels. But the Great Mughal eclipsed everyone. Keeping his habitual simplicity aside, he had pinned up on his turban the biggest ruby in the world surrounded by diamonds, which held his crest of feathers. Around the neck and arms were strings of emeralds, pearls and diamonds. His sword was incrusted with enormous emeralds. Even his Turkish slippers with their upturned tips, bore rubies and pearls. He took his seat on his throne completely covered in gold, incrusted with the biggest tailpiece of emerald and rubies, the back of which was depicted a peacock fanning its tail, the bird being the symbol of royalty in India.

The embassy was introduced with the sound of drums and trumpets. Jean recognized the Portuguese uniform of the officers. They were in large numbers, with a few Jesuits amongst them, indispensable to the Portuguese presence, led by the count of Minas, a great lord dressed all in black, his collar tightly encircled in a large white ruff, around the neck wearing the heavy necklace of l'Ordre de la Toison d'Or (the Order of the Golden Fleece). Jean could not suppress his amazement and joy at recognizing the tall height, thinness, and nonchalant air of Rodrigo Aveiro! Despite the thirty-five years that had passed since their separation, Jean found the same drooping eyes, the wearied expression, and the disillusioned smile, which hid one of the sharpest smiles. Rodrigo's eyes stopped at him and he recognized him at the very first look. A narrow smile appeared on his thin lips. None of this was missed by the Great Mughal who announced: 'To honour our illustrious visitors even more, today it will be my loyal collaborator, Jean, the Prince of Bourbon, who shall assure the translation.'

The ambassador, after having offered homage to the Great Mughal, delivered his speech. He assured Akbar of the unfailing friendship of his master, the King of Portugal who, to prove his feelings, could not be more willing to develop commercial relations between the two empires. Rodrigo spoke for a long time and seemed prodigiously bored of his own speech. Jean translated that in Persian just as he translated in French Akbar's response prepared in advance. Then the latter entrusted the ambassador and his suite to the care of the superintendent of the palace, in other words Jean, before he withdrew.

With all necessary ceremony, Jean led the Portuguese to the palace of the privileged guests. A gala banquet took place in the big hall of the palace with pink sandstone walls. Filigree of the same stone masked the windows, the floor was made of big slabs of white marble covered in Persian carpets. The Portuguese took their seats, not without awkwardness, on the low divans with round tables in front of which a horde of servants came and laid the items of the banquet. They could not see their compatriots, Julia and her sister Maria, the king's Christian wife, who were in a mezzanine placed very high and protected from everyone's eyes by a white marble mashrabiya, who along with other ladies of the harem were watching the spectacle. There were dozens of dishes of Indian cuisine, each more succulent than the next. The Portuguese did honour to the strong alcohol served to them. When the nautch girls, the official dancers, performed their mystic yet erotic dances, their enthusiasm knew no bound. They all found themselves, Jesuits included, in a rather elevated state.

Only Jean and Rodrigo maintained their sobriety, finally being able to give up their official distance and chat like long-lost friends. Jean had really not been expecting to see him again so suddenly. Rodrigo, however, had known he was going to meet his friend again: Father Marilva, who had succeeded in returning to Portugal, had spoken enough about him to those who wanted to listen. This French adventurer, supposedly a prince, this ignoble traitor, this despicable renegade, this sworn enemy of Portugal and the Portuguese continues to be the all-powerful favourite of the Great Mughal, controlling him undoubtedly with the help of witchcraft, black magic and other dark arts. Rodrigo made the neighing sound that served as a laugh as he sketched the picture that the Jesuit had drawn of Jean. He added: 'No one listens to him. Despite his saber rattling, the truth about him was discovered. He is disgraced.' Then he narrated his own story. He had abandoned the military for diplomacy, which led him to the highest responsibilities of the State. He had thus led several missions in foreign countries.

Jean, in his turn, described his adventures since their separation. He recounted in detail his relationship with Father Marilva, the abominations that the latter had finally been accused of, which did not quite surprise Rodrigo. 'But,' Jean questioned, 'by what miracle, my dear Rodrigo, do you now call yourself the count of Minas?'

'Quite simply, because many members of my family died without leaving behind any descendants. And this has left me as the only contender of our hereditary title. But my dear Jean, do explain to me why you present yourself now as the Prince of Bourbon? You had spoken in Ethiopia about the possibility that you could be the son of the commander of the same name, but at that time you were not certain. Pardon me my indiscretion and my insolence, but have you disguised yourself with this illustrious origin so as to convince the Great Mughal to employ you?'

'It is not the Great Mughal,' replied Jean, 'who needed convincing, but I. Over the course of these years, I began slowly, and so to speak unconsciously, forging the belief that I truly was the legitimate son of the Commander. I thus took on my filiations, at a time when, contrary to what you are implying, it was of no use to me. In fact, when I arrived at this court, believe me that no one, amongst the Indians, had the slightest idea about the Maison de France and the Bourbon family. They had vaguely heard of the kingdom of Francici, the French, but they knew nothing about all the kings who reigned there. Moreover, the empire was not yet solidly established. Threats and dangers surrounded the so very young emperor. He had other worries than to find out the significance of the name Bourbon.

'When I met Akbar for the first time, he had, in spite of his young age, acquired through trials, a surprising maturity. The piercing eyes that he fixed on me as I narrated my story to him unveiled to him who I really was. Believe me, if I had lied or fabricated a false identity, then he would have immediately caught on. One does not deceive Akbar when he is approaching his fifties. One did not deceive Akbar when he was seventeen years old. It is he who, because of the faith he had in me, convinced me of my identity.'

'But then, Jean, if you really are the Commander's son then why have you not claimed your rights and retrieved your heritage?'

'I must confess to you that I have had vague desires, not so much for myself as for my sons. But reason swept it away. Too many years have passed. For me, everything is over as far as France is concerned because nothing ever started there. The Commander was held a traitor; I do not wish to arouse bad memories by declaring myself his son. I have made peace with the Valois.[3] They may keep the inheritance that they stole from me and continue to rule gloriously.'

'But there are no more Valois,' exclaimed Rodrigo, 'the Valois are dead, they are finished! The last of the dynasty, King Henri III, was assassinated hardly a year ago, and he left no children. This crown was to automatically pass on to the closest male relative who turned out to be a distant cousin, Henri de Bourbon, today Henri IV.'

Suddenly, very excited, Jean raised his voice, in front of the other Portuguese staggering around because of the streams of alcohol, infatuated by the swaying hips of the nautch girls: 'I am older than Henri de Bourbon, thus today, it is I, the chief of the Maison de France. It should be me on that throne of France instead of him!' He gave out a laugh that was partly ironic and partly sad, and then was lost in his thoughts. Rodrigo watched him with half-closed eyes and spoke to him in a soft voice: 'The king of Portugal, my master, will be happy to help you ascend the throne of France which belongs to you.'

'The king of Portugal!' exclaimed Jean, 'but my dear Rodrigo, there is no king.'

The Jesuits of the mission had indeed told him about the events that had shaken Portugal. The reigning dynasty had fallen apart when King Sebastian disappeared in Morocco without a descendant. His closest relative, the king of Spain, the son of a Portuguese princess, invaded and occupied the country. Rodrigo made a nonchalant gesture. 'Supposing the king of Spain, having a strict sense of right and justice, is ready to put on the throne of France its legitimate heir.'

'The king of Spain, like his father emperor Charles Quint, has only one thing on his mind, to destroy France. The father had used my father. The son is waiting to use his son. He wants me to forcibly take the French crown. He wants me to follow the example of my father, and surrounded by the enemies of my homeland, wage war on France. It is enough that there had been one traitor in my family. I prefer to disregard my rights so as to earn forgiveness for my father. I just wish that France continues to ignore me.'

Rodrigo didn't let go so easily. He used all the arguments that his brilliant intelligence suggested to him. 'But my dear Rodrigo,' Jean interrupted, 'you are forgetting that I already own a kingdom. Evidently Shergar is not France, but it is completely enough for me.' Rodrigo talked about Henri IV's weakness, the division of France between catholic and heretic Protestants. He said that Henri IV had not hesitated to renounce the religion they had shared in order to climb the rickety throne of France. 'It won't take much,' concluded Rodrigo, 'for France, under your guidance, to go back to the true religion.' Jean gave out a small laugh: 'My dear Rodrigo, you are the worthy successor of Father Marilva. I almost felt I was listening to him! Perhaps you came here on his instigation. He did not succeed in turning me into his handy man next to the Great Mughal. Perhaps the only reason you came here was to attempt to place on the French throne your friend, turned into a puppet for you and your master. Unfortunately, you must look for another candidate...'

Rodrigo still refused to admit defeat: 'What a pity, you could have been of such use to France!' Jean made a lethargic gesture: 'Even if I were young, I would not have followed you. You see Rodrigo, France rejected me, Akbar trusted me and gave me a new life. India welcomed me with open arms and gave me a whole new life, allowing me to finally make peace with myself. I am far too grateful to him to abandon him. I hope that my descendants assume their French and royal ancestry, and as a reminder to them, I will hand down to them the only possession that came to me from the Commander, this bag of gunpowder with his arms on it. But more than anything I want to be an Indian. My past is closed, only the future interests me, our future is in India, as India is the future.' He got up with the weightlessness of a young man: 'Rodrigo, we must now part without any resentment.'

'Without resentment, Jean,' the ambassador replied fatalistically.

Jean de Bourbon died soon after the Portuguese ambassador's visit to the Great Mughal's court. The exact date of his death was never found, but he had crossed his seventieth year. He was buried in the small cemetery adjacent to the church that he had built in Agra. Many years later, his wife Julia joined him there. Her sister,

Maria, on the other hand, was buried next to the magnificent tomb of her husband, the Great Mughal, Akbar, in Sikandra, north of Agra.

1 A turban brooch
2 Hindu and Muslim rulers of vassal states
3 François I and his descendants

Postscript

The eldest son of Jean and Julia, Saviel de Bourbon, inherited the post of his father and became the superintendent of the palace. As for the younger one, Charles, there is practically no information available about him. For four generations, the descendants of Jean de Bourbon served the descendants of the Great Mughal Akbar, occupying high positions in the court.

Then came the decline of the empire, divisions weakened it, scheming and plotting ate into it. The powerful Shah of Persia took advantage of the situation: he invaded India and in 1739, captured the capital Delhi as well as the then Great Mughal. He seized the fabulous treasures gathered by the kings over generations. He took to Persia the jewels that were worn by Akbar, the famous peacock throne on which he sat and which would never be seen again. The Bourbons now felt themselves to be of no use to the descendants of Akbar. They were threatened by the invaders as by their rivals in the court, and thus withdrew to their principality of Shergar.

Balthazar IV de Bourbon told me about all this. He knew practically nothing about the first of the family, Jean de Bourbon, but he was somewhat well informed about his descendants. 'Soon after,' he continued, 'a neighbouring raja who hated the Great Mughals and all those who had served them, attacked Shergar, captured it one Christmas night and offered to the Bourbons the choice of surrender or death. The latter refused to surrender and were all executed with their servants, starting with François de Bourbon, the head of the family, the great-great-grandson of Jean de Bourbon, who was more than sixty years old. Only his son, Salvator I, managed to escape and take temporary refuge in the city of Gwalior.'

In 1785, he chose to migrate to Bhopal. It was at a time when, taking advantage of the decomposition of the Mughal Empire, new principalities cropped up here and there, mainly in the centre and west of India. Bhopal was one of them. Some decades earlier, an Afghan adventurer had come and established this vast and powerful state. A Muslim, he assumed the title of nawab. Bhopal attracted other adventurers who were interested in making their fortunes.

Salvator, being one of them, soon acquired the post of the governor of the city fort. 'Salvator's son, Balthazar I de Bourbon, was, after the founder of the dynasty Jean de Bourbon, the second big man of the family,' recounts his descendant. At the beginning of the nineteenth century, the maharaja of Gwalior attacked Bhopal at the head of an army of eighty thousand men. Bhopal lined up a hundred thousand soldiers. This was enough for Balthazar to push back several attacks, and even to follow the attackers to Gwalior. The general-in-chief of the defeated army was so humiliated that he committed suicide by swallowing a diamond.

'A few years later, the maharaja of Gwalior attacked Bhopal again. At the head of an army that was even stronger this time around was a remarkable general in whom he had complete confidence, a Frenchman, Jean-Baptiste Filose. Once again, my ancestor Salvator was heading the meager troops of Bhopal. Soldiers of both armies lined up on the battlefield, ready to throw themselves on one another. The two generals-in-chief waited to see who gave the first signal. Suddenly, Salvator de Bourbon moved towards Jean-Baptiste Filose and proposed a duel with him in order to avoid a massacre. He preferred the death of a general-in-chief over that of thousands of victims. Filose drew his sword and threw it to the ground. "We both are sons of France, why should we be fighting one another?" The two generals, instead of battling each other to death, embraced each other, exchanged their helmets, swore eternal friendship and both returned back to their homes. Balthazar had become the hero of Bhopal.'

Some years hence, the ruler of Bhopal, the nawab died, killed by a mysterious pistol shot, probably an accident. He left behind only one wife, Kudsia Begum, and a daughter aged four years, Sikander Begum. Immediately after, candidates for the throne started pouring in, cousins, nephews, and rivals. Balthazar imposed the fatherless Sikander on it with the widow Kudsia Begum as the regent of her daughter. These women needed solid support and found it in the man who had put them on the throne, Salvator. His power was greater than ever. It got better with Balthazar falling madly in love with the regent, Kudsia Begum. This adoration was shared, in spite of all the difficulties imposed by a life in purdah.

Balthazar I had a grandiose palace built in the city, the Shaukat Mahal. I have been there, it spreads over several hectares and comprises such large courtyards that they were opened to the intense traffic of the city. The architecture and the decoration is not really Indian but rather inspired by European baroque. Balthazar IV told me how the family lost the palace:

'Barely had it been completed that Balthazar invited Kudsia Begum to visit Shaukat Mahal. On arriving she was ecstatic: she had never seen a place so beautiful. Balthazar leaned forward towards the empress, "The palace is for you, madam." And he not only offered her the palace but also all that it contained. Meanwhile, the exchange of messages and fleeting rendezvous between the lovers had turned into a scandalous affair between a Muslim empress and her Christian prime minister. To protect the reputation of his beloved, Balthazar returned to Delhi and in 1823, at the age of forty-nine, married with great pomp in the cathedral a ravishing adolescent blond of fifteen years, Isabelle, daughter of an English noble. Their return to Bhopal was celebrated like a national festival. Kudsia Begum, who was now twenty-four years old, conferred on her rival the title of Madam Dulhan Sircar, and an unexpected friendship was established between these two women who loved the same man.

'But Balthazar's enemies, the Afghan nobles who he had removed from power, were watching. He survived a few conspiracies, but they succeeded in poisoning him. His body sweated through each of his pores and he vomited on his richly embroidered black clothes. Doctors were consulted, they used an antidote in vain, and he like others knew that the dew of death had been placed on his forehead.'

He left behind a widow of twenty-five years, Isabelle. She automatically became the head of the family. She expended as much energy as she did authority and lived strongly for a long time. It was her that Louis Rousselet visited in 1865, she had preserved the favour of the begums and succeeded in expanding the already considerable fortune of the family. She employed more than six thousand servants, and when she died in 1882 at the age of seventy-six, she passed on an unbelievable amount of jewels, a hundred houses in Bhopal, forty elephants, two trading houses and six thousand golden rupees to each of her numerous grand children. Kudsia Begum, mistress of her husband, and Sikander Begum, Kudsia's daughter, died before her.

Shahjehan Begum ruled from now on. Contrary to her mother and her grandmother, she hated the Bourbons and the Christians. She didn't dare do anything as long as Isabelle de Bourbon was alive, whose popularity she dreaded. But the old woman had barely been buried that she closed the church built by her and chased the Christians from Bhopal. While she was at it, she abolished the annual tribute paid to the Bourbons by the reigning dynasty.

After Shahjehan Begum, her daughter, Sultanjahan, succeeded the throne, the last of these astonishing sovereigns, the only women to have hereditarily occupied a Muslim throne. The new sovereign did better than her mother: she simply confiscated the fortune of the Bourbons. The head of the family then was Bonaventure de Bourbon, the great-grandchild of the illustrious Balthazar and princess Isabelle. Overnight, he was on the street with his family. Three to four hundred members of the Bourbon clan, no longer able to provide for themselves, migrated out of India, as was already told to me by Balthazar IV. The only one who stayed was Bonaventure and his immediate descendants. It was around this time that the bag of gunpowder bearing the Commander's arms that many eyewitnesses claimed to have seen in the possession of the Bourbons of Bhopal, disappeared.

One had to wait for India's independence and the limitation of power of the sovereigns, nawabs and maharajas, for Salvator II of Bourbon, son of Bonaventure, to reclaim some of his familial fortune.

Balthazar IV, who received me was the son of this Salvator II and the grandson of Bonaventure. Like his father and his grandfather, he proved to be extremely discreet about the rift between the Bourbons and the Begums and all that was suffered by the Bourbons. He preferred to forget this phase of the past, sad and miserable, and instead think about, with a smile on his lips, the future that included his three beautiful children.

Fourteen generations separated him from the founder of the family, the legendary Jean de Bourbon. Amongst the men, Balthazar is the eldest of his descendants; he has thus inherited his rights. If Jean de Bourbon was actually the son of the Commander, as he eventually came to believe, his descendant Balthazar IV de Bourbon would be the eldest of the Maison de France... if not the last.

References

The Bourbons of Bhopal exist, I have met them. The identity papers of these Indian nationals all bear the prestigious name Bourbon. It was the French traveller Rousselet who first introduced them to the West. Passing by Bhopal in 1865, he met Princess Isabelle de Bourbon, widow of Balthazar I. Questioned by him on the origins of her family, she succinctly recounted the life of Jean de Bourbon to him: 'During the reign of the great Akbar, around about 1557 or 1559, a European called Jean de Bourbon came to the Court in Delhi. He said he was French and belonged to one of the noblest families of the country. He said while travelling with his tutor, he was taken prisoner by Turkish pirates and was brought in captivity to Egypt. This event took place in 1541, when he was fifteen years old. Once in Egypt, the young man, because of his qualities, won the favour of the sovereign who incorporated him in his army. In a war against the Abyssinians, he was once taken prisoner. His Christian identity, his intelligence, his education won him a certain position in this country. It made it possible for him, under some pretext, to get to the Indian coast on one of the Abyssinian vessels which, at that time, had constant contact with the west coast of this country. Disembarking in Broach, he heard of the splendour of the Great Mughal's Court. He deserted the fleet of the Abyssinians and made his way to Agra. Emperor Akbar, to whom the young European narrated his story, was so won over by the elegance of his mannerisms, his intelligent appearance that he offered him a position in his army. Soon after, he appointed him the head of the artillery. Loaded with honours and wealth, prince Jean de Bourbon died in Agra, leaving two sons...'

In her short recital, Princess Isabelle gave precisely the stages of Jean de Bourbon's odyssey. She was not the only one in India to talk about him. Colonel W. Kincaid, a former Indian political servant, published in the *Asiatic Quarterly Review* of January 1887: 'In the second half of the sixteenth century, around 1560, Jean de Bourbon from Navarre, member of the youngest branch of the family of Henri IV, left for India on a boat, according to tradition. He was forced to leave France, because he had in a duel killed a relative of a high rank. He arrived in Madras where the emperor sent for him, and interested by his story, he treated him with great fondness and distinction.'

Mesrob Jacob Seth, a gold medalist from Calcutta University, member of the Asiatic Society of Bengal and of the Royal Asiatic Society of Great Britain and of Ireland, wrote, in his work *Armeniens in India from the Earliest Time to the Present Days,* in chapter 5: 'During the reign of the illustrious Akbar, rightly nicknamed the Great, there arrived in the Court of the Mughal, between 1557 and 1559, a French prince, Jean Philippe Bourbon of Navarre, originally from the Royal House of France. He told the emperor that he had been captured by the Turkish pirates during a voyage that he was on with his family's priest, his tutor, and was brought a prisoner to Egypt. Once there, the young man soon won the respect of the king by his affable behaviour. The latter took him in his service and gave him the post of command in his army. During a war against the Abyssinians, he was once again captured but, because he was Christian, rose to high positions in this Christian country. Because of his high position, he managed under some pretext to sail to India in one of those Abyssinian vessels, which, in that epoch, maintained regular relations with the Konkan coast. Having heard of the splendour and the reigning munificence in the Court of the Great Mughal, he deserted the Abyssinian fleet and rushed to Agra. Akbar who always received well the foreigners of distinction in his Court, was struck by the graceful manners, intelligent bearing and spirit of Jean. He immediately offered him a commanding post in his army. One year later, he appointed him the master of cannons ...'

The Begum of Bhopal, Sultana Jahan, the first to take in the Bourbons, published about Balthazar I in the annals of her dynasty: 'Hakim Shahzad Masih (the Indian name of Balthazar I) was a descendant of a Frenchman, Jean Philippe de Bourbon, one of the adventurers worthy of interest and who was believed to belong to the royal family of France and came to India during Akbar's reign. He served in Akbar's army and his son became an officer of the artillery.'

In the sixties of the last century, a polish traveller, Vitold de Golish, who visited nawabs and maharajas, as Rousselet had done a century earlier, arrived in Bhopal and by chance met Salvator de Bourbon, grandfather of the present Balthazar IV. He recounted the origin of their family: 'He, Jean-Philippe de Bourbon, is the founder of our House in India. It is he who, having left Pau in the sixteenth century, arrived in India after a long adventurous voyage. Being admitted in the service of the Great Mughal Akbar, who asked him to organize his artillery, he became his friend and received the title of maharaja of several cities, sixty villages and twenty castles. He died honourable and rich. He had two sons.'

Despite the discrepancies of these accounts, they are a proof of the fact that there was a European, a Frenchman, who called himself Jean de Bourbon, who appeared in the court of the Great Mughal Akbar and was hired by the same.

The question that researchers ask themselves is evidently to know if this Jean de Bourbon was hanging on to the family tree of the House of France. Several hypotheses were put down, each more unlikely than the next.

Rousselet, once again, put me on the right path. In the second edition of (1879) of his *Inde des rajahs* (India of the Rajas), an unedited paragraph, missing from the first edition of 1875 put me on track: 'I leave it to whomsoever be interested in the matter to decide whether this Jean Philippe de Bourbon was a part of the French family of the Bourbons, and if this were true, he wasn't an illegitimate son of the famous Commander who lived during that time, or if he was nothing but an imposter.'

Why Rousselet liked this hypothesis, no one knows, but he must have had some reasons for doing so. In *Les annals bourbonnaises* of 1892, he wrote: 'There exists in Bourbonnais a legend that says that the Commander de Bourbon had left a son who was sent to India to protect him from the rancor of François I.'

However, it seemed unlikely that one of the most important figures in Christianity could have had a legitimate son without it being known. I had thus put together the hypothesis that I developed in this piece of work. Apart from her uncontrollable passion for the Commander of Bourbon, Louise de Savoie wanted at all costs to get her hands on her cousin's, the Duchess Suzanne's, inheritance. She had already proven that she did not stop at anything. Her son and her descendants were ready for any amount of dishonesty to keep this fortune that she had unjustly acquired. The hiding of the legitimate heir is thus explained, and it is not the only example in history.

Rousselet, after the success of his *L'Inde des rajahs*, published in 1882 another work, not an account of travels, but a book titled *Le Fils du Connétable* (The Commander's Son). Speaking in the first person, these false memoirs narrate the story of Jean de Bourbon since his childhood. Treated by some as pure fiction, and besides being garnished by historical errors, this work which concerns Jean de Bourbon very often sounds true, because of which I think that Rousselet, in writing this, had access to unknown sources. Believing in the veracity of his sayings, I was inspired. It is not *Le Fils du Connétable*, but the second edition of *L'Inde des rajahs* where Rousselet recounts: 'The respected missionary who attended our meeting (with Isabelle de Bourbon), assured me that there was in the family treasure an escutcheon bearing fleurs de lys, crudely painted, belonging to Jean Philippe de Bourbon.'

This family souvenir must necessarily have been of a small size for Jean de Bourbon to have carried it through all his adventures. I thus imagined the bag of gunpowder given by the Commander, which confirms that the child had at least once met his presumed father.

The capture by Turkish pirates, and the service in the Egyptian army are episodes which one finds in the framework of Jean de Bourbon's life told by others than Rousselet.

The stay in Ethiopia and the achievement of high positions was found/covered in the works of other authors than Rousselet. Incidentally, Rousselet had been mistaken about the name of the Ethiopian emperor as well as the state of the empire. It wasn't easy for me to reestablish the truth.

The Portuguese, in that epoch, had infiltrated the Ethiopian empire and had occupied a large part of the west coast of India. It was easy for me to imagine Jean de Bourbon entering their service, particularly in the service of the Jesuits, the fifth column of Lusitanian imperialism.

Researchers agree on the dates from 1550 to 1560 for the arrival of Jean de Bourbon in Akbar's court. It could not have been before since Akbar, then a very young man, only came to power in 1560.

On the other hand, Jean, the legitimate son of the Commander, couldn't have been born after 1521, the date of the death of the Duchess Suzanne. He must have thus been in his forties when he presented himself to the Great Mughal. From the moment he arrived in the court of the latter, the existence of Jean de Bourbon is better documented. There is no doubt about the fact that Akbar had instantly trusted him, hired him and appointed him the head of artillery. The fact the Julia Mascarenhas was the second wife of Jean is also firmly established.

In 1903, Ismail Gracias de Goa, member of the Royal Academy of Lisbon, published a brochure *A Portuguese lady à la Cour du Grand Moghol*: 'The alleged Christian wife of Akbar was one of the sisters who, during the second half of the sixteenth century, were sent from a royal orphanage of Lisbon to Goa to be married there. This is a known custom. The vessel on which they were travelling was captured by a Dutch boat and the sisters were taken to Surat and sold to the court of the Great Mughal. Akbar himself married the elder one and made Julia, the younger one, the harem's doctor. What is more, he finally gave Julia in marriage to a certain Jean Philippe de Bourbon, a relative of Henri IV of France.'

Mesrob Jacob Seth wrote: 'Worried about attaching the prince (Jean) to his court in a permanent fashion, Akbar gave him in marriage an Armenian woman by the name of Julia, who was employed as a doctor, with the medical responsibility of Akbar's harem.' It is not incomprehensible that the author had made the Portuguese into an Armenian, himself belonging to the same glorious race.

Colonel Kincaid added: 'Being very happy with his courteous manners and his conduct, he wanted to keep his services and offered him in marriage Dame Julia, sister of Akbar's Christian wife, who, thanks to her talent and her knowledge of European medicine, was in charge of the health of the imperial wives. This marriage was duly celebrated and after that Akbar conferred upon his brother-in-law the title of Nawab Masih, and placed the responsibility of the imperial seraglio under him. Dame Julia was included in the very close group of imperial sisters. The honourable responsibility conferred upon the Bourbons remained in the family till the pillage of Delhi by Nadir Shah in 1739.'

Mesrob Jacob Seth, who made Julia into an Armenian compatriot, specified: 'This dame who, according to certain authors, was the sister of the Christian wife of Akbar, had built the first Christian church in Agra, where, according to tradition founded on the Bourbon registers in India, Dame Julia and Jean Philippe de Bourbon were buried.'

Later on, this church was demolished but the registers still exist in the archives of Agra. The documentation referring to Jean de Bourbon is found in a remarkable piece of work called *Les Bourbons de l'Inde,*[1] whose author, Lucien Jailloux, after exhaustive research on the subject, brought to light the life of Salvatore de Bourbon, the grandfather of the actual Balthazar IV.

The adventures of the Bourbons of India after Jean, the founder of the dynasty, are an integral part of the history of India. Some suppose that Jean de Bourbon had quite simply borrowed this illustrious name and was nothing more than an impostor. I do not see why he would have done that, since, in any case at that time, the Bourbons were unknown in India. Moreover, Akbar was perspicacious enough to see through an impostor in his entourage.

Others are amazed that the Bourbons in India, if they really belonged to the House of France, never tried to establish contact with the latter. Jean de Bourbon was always torn about the fact that the Commander was a traitor. And this is why, all his life, he hesitated to come to France, or even establish a contact with the country of his origin. This was also the reason why he wished that his descendants, in spite of their illustrious origin, be exclusively Indian, which they remain till today.

1 Christian Edition, 2003.

Acknowledgements

I would like to thank those who have helped me in the course of writing this work:

Balthazar and Elisha and their children.

Nicolas Foin

The countess Boulay de la Meurthe

Sébastien de Courtois

Chantal de Batz

Madame Odile de Crépy

Charlotte Cachin Liebert

And Marina, who with untiring patience read and re-read my manuscript in order to correct it better.

Index